MACMILLAN
INTERMEDI

VIKAS SWARUP

Slumdog Millionaire

Retold by John Escott

MACMILLAN

MACMILLAN READERS

INTERMEDIATE LEVEL

Founding Editor: John Milne

The Macmillan Readers provide a choice of enjoyable reading materials for learners of English. The series is published at six levels – Starter, Beginner, Elementary, Pre-intermediate, Intermediate and Upper.

Level Control
Information, structure and vocabulary are controlled to suit the students' ability at each level.

The number of words at each level:

Starter	about 300 basic words
Beginner	about 600 basic words
Elementary	about 1100 basic words
Pre-intermediate	about 1400 basic words
Intermediate	about 1600 basic words
Upper	about 2200 basic words

Vocabulary
Some difficult words and phrases in this book are important for understanding the story. Some of these words are explained in the story, some are shown in the pictures, and others are marked with a number like this: ...^{3}. Words with a number are explained in the *Glossary* at the end of the book.

Answer Keys
Answer Keys for the *Points for Understanding* and *Exercises* sections can be found at www.macmillanenglish.com/readers.

Contents

	A Note About The Author	4
	A Note About The Story	5
	The Places In This Story	8
	The People In This Story	9
1	Cheat!	10
2	Father Timothy	13
3	A Home for the Disabled	16
4	Tragedy Queen	26
5	A Soldier's Story	32
6	A Brother's Promise	40
7	How to Speak Australian	46
8	Murder on a Train	55
9	A Love Story	60
10	At Home with a Killer	73
11	Look after your Buttons	78
12	The Last Question	82
13	A Sister's Promise	88
	Points for Understanding	91
	Glossary	96
	Exercises	102

A Note About The Author

Vikas Swarup was born in Allahabad in India. After going to the Allahabad Boys' High School and College, Vikas went on to study psychology[1], history and philosophy[2] at Allahabad University. In 1986, he joined the Indian Foreign Service. As a diplomat[3], he worked in Turkey, the United States of America, Ethiopia, Great Britain and South Africa. In August 2009, he became Consul General of India in Osaka, Japan.

Q and A – the title of the book which was made into the film *Slumdog Millionaire* – was his first book. It took him only two months to write, but has now been published in forty-two different languages and made into a very successful film. He has written a second novel, *Six Suspects*, which was published in 2008.

Vikas likes listening to music, playing cricket, tennis and table tennis. He is married to Aparna and they have two sons, Aditya and Varun.

For a detailed interview with Vikas Swarup, visit the student's section of the Macmillan Readers website at www.macmillanenglish.com/readers.

A Note About The Story

Vikas Swarup says that he got the idea for *Slumdog Millionaire* after watching the popular TV show, *Who Wants To Be A Millionaire?*. He thought that it would be interesting if an uneducated 'street boy' won the top prize – a boy who would definitely be accused[4] of cheating.

The TV show *Who Wants To Be A Millionaire?* has been seen in more than one hundred countries. It was first shown on ITV1 in the UK on 4th September, 1998. In March 1999, a record 19.2 million people watched the programme. The Indian version of the show started in 2000 and has been hosted[5] by Bollywood actors Amitabh Bachchan and Shahrukh Khan.

There have been special *Who Wants To Be A Millionaire?* programmes with teams of celebrities competing for charity[6] and, in some countries, children competing against one another for prizes for their schools.

Slumdog Millionaire tells the story of Ram Mohammad Thomas. Ram's name is given to him by Father Timothy, a Catholic priest[7]. The name brings together three important religions: Ram is from the Hindu religion, Mohammad from the Muslim religion and Thomas from Christianity. The characters in the story call the boy the name that matches their own religion. For example, Salim is Muslim, so he calls his friend Mohammad. Colonel Taylor is Christian, so he calls him Thomas and Smita the lawyer is Hindu, so she calls him Ram.

Ram is a young boy who was born in Delhi and grows up in the slums[8] of Mumbai. Mumbai, which was once called Bombay, is one of the biggest cities in the world. There have always been slums in the city, but now almost sixty per cent of its thirteen million people live in slum buildings, and the number is still growing. The biggest problem in the slums is the water supply. There is always too much or too little water. In the monsoon[9] season many slums are flooded, making living conditions even worse. Some people call the city 'Slumbay'.

Ram has his own reasons for getting on the TV show *Who Will Win a Billion?*, reasons that we only discover at the end of the book. After being accused of cheating, Ram tells his lawyer different stories about his life. Each story shows how he came to know the answers to the questions on the show.

The film of *Slumdog Millionaire* stars Dev Patel as the boy who grows up in the slums of Mumbai. It is a 2008 British film, directed by Danny Boyle, and was filmed in India. It was nominated[10] for ten Academy Awards – Oscars – in 2009 and won eight, including Best Picture and Best Director.

For more information on the film Slumdog Millionaire, *visit the student's section of the Macmillan Readers website at www.macmillanenglish.com/readers.*

People, places and events in the story:

Surdas
Surdas lived in the fifteenth century. He was a saint, poet and musician. He was born in a small village in India. He could not see. It is thought that he left his family at the age of six, when he followed a group of singers who were passing through the village. Surdas was a very religious man and wrote over one hundred thousand poems, though only around eight thousand can be found today.

India and Pakistan
At the start of the twentieth century, India was part of the British Empire. Then, in 1947, two separate, independent countries were created – India and Pakistan. But the neighbouring countries had many troubles. There were violent wars in 1947, 1965 and 1971.

The Taj Mahal

The Taj Mahal, often called the Taj, was built by Emperor Shahjahan. Work started in 1631 and took twenty-two years. Shahjahan, who was called Prince Khurram before he became emperor, had fallen in love with a beautiful woman. He called her Mumtaz Mahal, which meant 'the chosen one'. They got married and had fourteen children. However, Mumtaz Mahal died while giving birth to the last child in 1631. Before she died, her husband promised to build the most beautiful palace in the world for her. The result was the Taj Mahal. Today, it is often described as one of the wonders of the world, and the palace receives up to four million visitors each year.

A glossary of Indian words:

rupee the unit of money used in India, Pakistan and some other countries such as Nepal. The short form of rupee is Rp or Rs. In India, you can get the following coins and notes: 1, 2, 5, 10, 20, 50, 100, 500 and 1000. Rs. 100 are equal to approximately £1.20, €1.40 or $2.00.

chapatti a type of thin flat Indian bread

sari a very long wide piece of cloth, especially silk, that women in India wrap around their bodies to make a type of long dress

chawl a large building with a lot of small rooms for people to rent in India, particularly in Mumbai. There are normally four or five floors in the building, with approximately fifteen rooms on each floor. There is usually a shared bathroom on each floor.

tiffin a small meal that you eat in the middle of the day or a small snack

The Places In This Story

The People In This Story

Ram Mohammad Thomas – a poor boy who wins *Who Will Win a Billion?*
Smita Shah – a young lawyer
Prem Kumar – the host of *Who Will Win a Billion?*
Salim Ilyasi – Ram's best friend

Delhi

Father Timothy – a Catholic priest
Mr Agnihotri – works at Delhi Children's Home for Boys
Mr Gupta – works at Delhi Children's Home for Boys
a fortune-teller

Colonel Taylor – an Australian diplomat
Rebecca Taylor – his wife
Roy Taylor – their son
Maggie Taylor – their daughter
Jeevan Kumar – works for the Indian government
the Australian high commissioner
servants, cooks and gardeners
policemen

Akshay – a boy on the train
Meenakshi – a girl on the train
their parents
a robber

Mumbai

Inspector Godbole – a police inspector
Sethji – a gangster whose real name is Babu Pillai, also called Maman
Mustafa – works for Maman
Punnoose – works for Maman
Masterji – a music teacher
some guards and beggars

Neelima Kumari – a famous actress
some cooks and maids

Balwant Singh – an old soldier
Mr Ramakrishna – the chawl manager
Mr Shantaram – a new resident in the chawl
Mrs Shantaram – his wife
Gudiya Shantaram – their daughter
residents from the chawl

Ahmed Khan – Salim's boss
Prakash Rao – a customer in a bar

Agra

Shankar – an orphan
Swapna Devi – a rich woman
Lajwanti – a maid
Nita – Ram's girlfriend
Nita's father
Utpal Chatterjee – a father and an English teacher
tourists and dinner guests

1
Cheat!

There is pain coming from every part of my body. I am hanging from a wooden beam[11] in a large room. My hands are tied to the beam with rope and my feet are a metre above the floor. Inspector Godbole has been hitting me for more than an hour. Earlier, he pushed my head into some water and held it there. I nearly drowned.

Now he is holding a pen and a piece of paper in front of me. The words on the paper say:

I, Ram Mohammad Thomas, cheated on the quiz show Who Will Win a Billion? *and I will not take my prize or any other prize. I am very sorry.*

Inspector Godbole wants me to sign my name on the paper. It is not true, I did not cheat on the show, but the television company cannot afford to pay me a billion rupees.

The pain is terrible. I cannot stand much more of it.

Suddenly, I hear voices shouting. Then a young woman comes into the room. She has long black hair and nice teeth. She is carrying a brown bag.

'Who are you?' shouts Godbole.

'My name is Smita Shah,' the woman tells him. 'I'm Mr Ram Mohammad Thomas' lawyer.' She looks at my body hanging from the beam, then she quickly looks away. 'This is against the law,' she says. 'Stop it now!'

Godbole is very surprised. So am I. I have never seen this woman before. And I cannot afford to pay for a lawyer.

'His lawyer?' says Godbole. 'You're his lawyer?'

'I'm Mr Ram Mohammad Thomas' lawyer.'

'Yes,' she says. 'I want to see the papers for his arrest[12]. Give them to me now, or I'll take Mr Thomas from the police station to talk with him privately.'

'Er ... I ... I'll have to speak to ... to the Commissioner,' says Godbole. 'Please wait.'

Then he hurries from the room.

I do not know when Godbole returns to the room. By then I have fainted[13] – from pain, hunger and happiness.

It is late evening. I am at Smita's house in Bandra, a very nice part of Mumbai. I have eaten and slept, and now I am sitting on a large sofa in her sitting room. Smita is sitting with me on the edge of the sofa. She is holding a DVD.

'I've got a DVD of the quiz show,' she says. 'Now we can look at it carefully. How were you able to answer all those questions? Did you cheat? You must tell me the truth, Ram.'

'Can I trust her?' I ask myself. I take out my lucky one-rupee coin. 'Heads[14] I talk to her, tails I say goodbye.' I throw the coin into the air. It comes down on heads.

'I was lucky,' I say to Smita.

'Lucky?' she replies. 'You *guessed* the correct answers?'

'No, I didn't guess them,' I say. 'I knew them.'

'So why were you lucky?' she asks.

'I was lucky because he asked me *those* questions,' I say.

Smita is silent for a moment. Then she says, 'Begin with question one. And promise to tell me the truth.'

'I promise,' I say.

Smita takes the shiny DVD from its cover and puts it into the DVD player.

2
Father Timothy

I was found outside the Church of St Mary in Delhi eighteen years ago on Christmas Day. Who put me there and why? I do not know. But I lived at St Mary's Church orphanage[15] for two years before Father Timothy, a kind priest, gave me a home. He also gave me a name.

'I'll call the boy Ram Mohammad Thomas,' he said. 'That will make people of all religions happy to meet him.'

Father Timothy had a very large house near the church, which had a big garden full of fruit trees. He had lived in India for many years, but he was born in York, in the north of England. Three times a year, Father Timothy went to England to visit his mother. He taught me to speak English, and my six years with him were the happiest of my life.

Many street children came to the church gardens to play cricket and football, and I soon began to feel part of a big family.

Father Timothy taught me about the life of Jesus[16], and I learnt about other religions from the street children and their parents.

The church had coloured glass windows. Above the altar[17] was a large crucifix of Christ and the letters INRI. I often looked up at it as I sat and enjoyed the church music and I loved the Christmas tree at Christmas.

For the first few years of my life, I believed that Father Timothy was my real father. I was surprised to hear other people call him Father, and that I had so many brothers and sisters. Also, Father Timothy was white and I was not, and I found this strange. One day I asked him about it and he explained that I was an orphan child. For the first time I understood the

Father Timothy

difference between Father – which is what people call their priest – and a father of children in a family. That night, I cried myself to sleep.

Father Timothy was a wonderful priest. I saw him give money to poor people and visit the sick. He always had a smile on his face.

I was eight years old when he died. It was the worst day of my young life.

———

'It's a sad story, Ram,' Smita says to me now. 'What happened to you then?'

'I was sent to a children's home,' I say.

'I see,' she replies. She looks at me sadly for a moment. Then she says, 'Now tell me about the first question.' And she presses 'Play' on the DVD player. We sit and watch the first question from *Who Will Win a Billion?*

———

Prem Kumar was the quiz's presenter[18]. He whispered to me, 'For the first question, I'll ask you, "What do the letters FBI mean?" Have you heard of the FBI?'

'No,' I said.

'Listen, we want you to win a little money, so I can change the question,' he said.

I thought for a moment. 'I don't know about FBI, but I know INRI,' I said. 'It's written on the top of a crucifix in church.'

The quiz show began.

'Tonight we've got Mr Ram Mohammad Thomas in the studio, from our very own Mumbai,' Prem Kumar said. 'What do you do, Mr Thomas?'

'I'm a waiter at Jimmy's Bar and Restaurant,' I explained.

'I see. Well, Mr Thomas, you seem to have all the religions in your name so you may know the answer to this question.

'Here it comes, for one thousand rupees. What are the letters on a crucifix: a) IRNI, b) INRI, c) RINI or d) NIRI? Do you understand the question, Mr Thomas?'

'Yes,' I replied. 'The answer is B. INRI.'

'Are you absolutely sure?'

'Yes,' I said.

There was the sound of drums. The correct answer lit up on the screen.

'Absolutely correct!' said Prem Kumar. 'You have won one thousand rupees.'

3
A Home for the Disabled[19]

After Father Timothy died, I was sent to the Delhi Children's Home for Boys, in Turkman Gate. It was crowded, noisy and dirty. The classrooms had broken desks and the teachers had not taught for years. We ate in a room with long wooden tables, but the cook sold most of our meat to restaurants. We were given vegetables and thick, blackened chapattis.

The warden[20] was Mr Agnihotri. He was a kind old man, but Mr Gupta, his deputy[21], gave the orders. He carried a stick and hit us with it whenever he felt like it.

I soon knew many boys in the home. Some were younger, but most were older than me. After living with Father Timothy, the home was a terrible place for me. But I soon realized that it was a good home for many of the boys. They came from the slums of Delhi and Bihar, and faraway Nepal. I heard their stories of cruel parents, of aunts and uncles who hit them and took their money.

I became the boys' leader. Not because I was bigger, but because I could speak English. This impressed the warden and the other officials and teachers. And when I was sick, the doctor immediately put me in a room on my own. I had been enjoying my time in that room for more than two weeks when another bed was brought in. They told me that a new boy had arrived. He was carried in that afternoon, wearing a torn shirt and dirty torn shorts. And that was my first meeting with Salim Ilyasi.

Salim had curly black hair and a nice smile. He was only seven years old, but he had a clever mind and he asked lots of intelligent questions.

Salim and I became very good friends. We were both orphans, with no hope of finding a family. We both loved

A Home for the Disabled

watching films. Salim's favourite actor was Armaan Ali. When we moved out of the sick room, I got him a bed next to mine.

One beautiful spring day, Salim and I were taken on a day trip by a charity organization. We travelled on a bus all over Delhi, then we were taken to India Gate to see a big carnival. We were each given ten rupees to spend.

I wanted to go on the big wheel[22] but Salim pulled at my sleeve. He had seen another booth[23] which interested him. A sign next to it read: *Pandit Ramshankar Shastri, World-Famous Fortune-Teller*[24]. *Only Rs.10 a reading.* In the booth sat an old man with a white moustache.

'I want to show him my hand,' said Salim. 'It's only ten rupees.'

'OK,' I said. 'But I'm not giving my ten rupees to this old man.'

Salim paid his money and put out his hand. The fortune-teller looked at it. After a time, he said, 'I see a very good future for you.'

'Do you?' said Salim, pleased. 'What will I be?'

Mr Shastri closed his eyes for ten seconds, then opened them. 'You have a beautiful face,' he said. 'You will be a very famous actor.'

'Like Armaan Ali?' asked Salim, excitedly.

'Even more famous than Armaan Ali,' replied the fortune-teller. He turned to me. 'Do you want to show me your hand?'

'No, thank you,' I said, and I began to move away.

Salim stopped me. 'Mohammad, you have to show him your hand,' he said. 'Do it for me, please.'

So I gave the old man my ten rupees and held out my right hand. He looked at it for more than five minutes, then he made some notes.

'What's wrong?' asked Salim.

The fortune-teller shook his head. He did not look happy.

A Home for the Disabled

'You will have many problems,' he said. 'I can help you, but it will cost money.'

'How much?' I asked.

'Two hundred rupees,' he said. 'You could ask your father for the money. Is that his big bus?'

I laughed. 'We're not rich children,' I said. 'We're orphans from the Delhi Home for Boys. That bus doesn't belong to our father. You should have checked before telling us stories.'

Salim and I were walking away when the fortune-teller called to me. 'Listen,' he shouted. 'I want to give you something.'

I walked back and he gave me an old one-rupee coin.

'It's a lucky coin,' he said. 'Keep it. You will need it.'

Salim wanted an ice cream, but we had only one rupee and that would not buy us anything. Suddenly, I dropped the coin. When I bent down to pick it up, I saw that it was lying next to a ten-rupee note which someone had dropped. So Salim and I bought ice creams and I put the coin carefully into my pocket. It *was* a lucky coin.

———

From time to time, a big man came to the home. His name was Sethji. Some boys said that he was a very rich businessman with no children of his own. They said that he owned a school in Mumbai and took the cleverest boys from our home to teach. We all hoped that Sethji would take us to his school.

Mumbai is the centre of the film business, so Salim hoped that Sethji would take him and make him a film star. He was sure that the fortune-teller's words were going to come true.

Sethji arrived with two other men. He did not look like a businessman, he looked like a gangster[25]. The two men with him looked like gangsters, too. I learnt later that their names were Mustafa and Punnoose. Mr Gupta was also with them.

Sethji looked carefully at each boy. All of us smiled our best smiles. Salim had had a bath and put on his best clothes. When Sethji came to Salim, he stopped.

'It's a lucky coin,' he said. 'Keep it. You will need it.'

A Home for the Disabled

'What is your name?' Sethji asked.

'S ... Salim Ilyasi,' replied Salim.

'When did he arrive?' Sethji asked Gupta.

'About eleven months ago, from Chhapra in Bihar,' said Gupta. 'He is eight, and his family are all dead.'

'That's very sad,' said Sethji. 'But he's the kind of boy that I need.'

Gupta looked at Salim, then at me. 'What about him?' He pointed at me.

Sethji looked at me. 'He is too old,' he said.

'He is only ten,' said Gupta. 'His name is Thomas and he speaks very good English. If you take Salim, you must take Thomas, too. You don't have to pay for him. Buy one, get one free.'

Sethji spoke with the other two men, then he said. 'OK, I'll take them on Monday.'

Salim did not sleep that night because he was too excited.

We travelled by train from Delhi to Mumbai with Mustafa and Punnoose. Sethji travelled by plane. Mustafa and Punnoose slept most of the time. They told us very little about Sethji. They said that his real name was Babu Pillai, but everyone called him Maman. That meant 'Uncle' in the Malayalam language. Maman came from Kollam in Kerala, but had lived in Mumbai for a long time. He had a school for disabled children. Maman believed that disabled children were nearer to God. He also saved children from homes and gave them a future. At Maman's school, we would be taught wonderful things and would go on to have successful lives, they told us. By the end of the journey, I was sure that this was the best thing that had ever happened to me.

A taxi took us to Maman's house in Goregaon. It was not the big house that we had expected. It was a large old building with a small garden and a high wall around it. Two big men

A Home for the Disabled

were sitting outside the house, smoking. They had long, heavy sticks in their hands. Punnoose spoke to them quickly in the Malayalam language. It was obvious that they were guards.

We went into the house and from the window, Mustafa pointed to some sheds in the garden. 'That is Maman's school for disabled children,' he said. 'The other children live there, too.'

'I don't see any children,' I said.

'They are having job training,' Mustafa said. 'You will see them later.'

He took us to our room. It was small, with two beds and a long mirror on the wall. In the basement[26] of the house there was a bathroom that we could use. We seemed to be the only children who were living there.

Maman came to welcome us in the evening. Salim told him that he was excited to be in Mumbai and that he wanted to be a famous film star. Maman smiled. 'To be a film star, you must be able to sing and dance,' he said. 'Can you sing?'

'No,' said Salim.

'Don't worry,' said Maman. 'I will get a good music teacher to give you lessons.'

Salim almost kissed Maman, but he stopped himself.

Later we went to the school for dinner. There were long wooden tables, but Salim and I sat at a small table with Mustafa. Our food came before the other children arrived. It was hot and good to eat, much better than the food at the Delhi Home for Boys.

Then the other children started coming in. It was terrible to watch. I saw boys with no eyes, boys with no arms, boys with no legs. It was good that Salim and I had nearly finished our meal.

Three boys were standing in one corner of the room, watching the others eat.

'They are being punished[27] for not doing enough work,'

A Home for the Disabled

Mustafa said. 'Don't worry, they'll eat later.'

The music teacher came the next day. 'Call me Masterji,' he told us.

When Salim sang, we discovered that he had a good voice.

'Very good,' said Masterji. Then he turned to me and told me to sing. When I sang, Masterji put his fingers in his ears. 'I will have to work very hard with you,' he said.

Mustafa and Punnoose tried to stop us from talking with the boys in the disabled school, but Salim and I soon got to know some of them. We heard their sad stories, but we also began to learn the truth about Maman.

'We are not schoolchildren,' thirteen-year-old Ashok told us. 'We are beggars[28]. We beg in trains.'

'What happens to the money you earn?' I asked.

'We have to give it to Maman's men,' replied Ashok.

'So Maman is a gangster,' I said.

'Yes,' said Ashok. 'But he gives us two meals each day.'

I was shocked and worried, but Salim continued to believe that all would end well for us.

'Why were you punished today?' I asked ten-year-old Raju, who was blind[29].

'I didn't earn enough money,' he said. 'If you give Maman's men less than one hundred rupees, you don't get food. You go to bed hungry.'

We spoke to Radhey, an eleven-year-old with only one leg.

'Why are you never punished?' I asked him.

'It's a secret,' he said, 'so please don't tell anyone. There's an actress who lives in Juhu. When I don't earn enough, I go to her. She gives me food and money. Her name is Neelima Kumari. People say that she was once very famous.'

A Home for the Disabled

'What does she look like?' asked Salim.

'You can see that she was very beautiful when she was young,' said Radhey. 'But now she's getting old. She needs a servant. If I had two legs, I would run away from here and work for her.'

That night, I dreamt I went to a house in Juhu. A tall woman opened the door. But the woman in my dream was not Neelima Kumari. She was my mother. She wore a white sari. I couldn't see her face because the wind was blowing her long black hair across it. I started to say something, but then I discovered that I had no legs.

I woke up screaming.

Our music lessons were coming to an end and Masterji was very pleased with Salim.

'There is only one more lesson,' Masterji said. 'You must learn the songs of Surdas.'

'Who is Surdas?' asked Salim.

'He was a very famous singer and he wrote thousands of songs praising[30] Lord Krishna,' said Masterji. 'He was also blind.'

On the last day of our music lessons, Punnoose came into the room to talk with Masterji. They talked in quiet voices, then Punnoose paid Masterji some money. They left the room together.

Then I saw a hundred-rupee note lying on the floor. Punnoose must have dropped it. I was going to put it in my pocket, but Salim took it from me. 'We must give it back to Punnoose,' he said.

We went to Maman's office. When we were near the door, we heard Maman and Punnoose talking.

'So what did Masterji say?' Maman was asking Punnoose.

'The older boy is terrible, but the younger one is very good,' said Punnoose. 'He could earn four or five hundred a day.'

A Home for the Disabled

'And the other boy?' asked Maman. 'The tall one? What should we do with him?'

'If he doesn't get us a hundred each night, then he goes to bed hungry,' replied Punnoose.

'OK, send them out on the trains from next week,' said Maman. 'We will do it to them tonight, after dinner.'

I was very afraid after hearing these words. I quickly grabbed Salim's arm and pulled him back to our room.

'Salim, we have to escape from this place,' I cried. 'Something very bad is going to happen to us after dinner. We were taught the songs of Surdas because he was blind. And *we* are going to be blind too, so that we can beg on the trains. I am sure that all the disabled boys here have been blinded or had their arms and legs cut off by Maman and his gang.'

'But where will we go?' asked Salim. 'What will we do?'

'Remember the actress, Neelima Kumari? Radhey told us about her,' I said. 'She needs a servant. I have her address and I know the train that goes there.'

'Why don't we go to the police?' suggested Salim.

'Are you crazy?' I said. 'Whatever you do and wherever you go, *never* go to the police.'

We were inside the bathroom and Salim was trying to open the window. Upstairs, we could hear Maman's guards in our room.

'Hurry!' I said.

'I can't open it!' Salim whispered. He was very frightened.

Now we could hear the sound of feet coming down the stairs.

At last Salim got the window open. He climbed out, then he took my hand and pulled me through. Outside, the moon was bright in the sky.

A Home for the Disabled

Soon we were on a train going to Juhu. A small, thin boy who was about seven or eight years old came along the train. He walked with a stick and had a begging bowl. He was blind. He stopped near us and began to sing one of Surdas' most famous songs. When he finished the song, he held out his begging bowl. The other passengers on the train gave him nothing. Salim took something from his pocket and looked at me. I nodded. Then Salim dropped Punnoose's hundred-rupee note into the boy's begging bowl.

———

Smita is shaking her head. 'It is difficult to believe that there are people who can be so cruel to children,' she says.

Then Smita pushes 'Play' on the DVD player.

———

Prem Kumar looked at the camera. 'We now have the two-thousand-rupee question,' he said. He looked at me. 'Are you ready?'

'Ready,' I replied.

'Which God did Surdas, the blind singer, pray to: a) Ram, b) Krishna, c) Shiva or d) Brahma?'

The music began.

'B. Krishna,' I said.

'Are you absolutely sure?' he said.

'Yes,' I said.

There was the sound of drums. The correct answer lit up on the screen.

'Absolutely correct!' said Prem Kumar. 'You have won two thousand rupees.'

Prem Kumar smiled. I did not.

4
Tragedy Queen[31]

For three years, I worked in Neelima Kumari's flat in Juhu. It all began after Salim and I got off the train. We walked up to her flat and rang the doorbell. After a time, the door opened. A tall, beautiful lady stood in front of us.

'Who are you?' she asked.

'We are friends of Radhey,' I replied. 'He told us where you lived and said that you needed a servant. We have come for the job. We need food and a place to stay, and we promise to do anything that you ask.'

'I don't need two servants,' she said. 'Which one of you had the idea of coming to me for the job?'

Salim pointed at me. 'He did,' he said.

So I got the job.

Neelima Kumari's flat had five bedrooms. Neelima's bedroom was the biggest and had a very large bed. It also had a big TV, a DVD player and video recorder and a cupboard full of film magazines.

Each magazine had Neelima's picture on the front of it. She was once the most famous actress in India.

Neelima's mother lived with her. She was nearly eighty years old. There was a lady who came to cook the evening meal and a girl who came to do the washing. I did everything else. I cleaned the house, made tea and went shopping. But Neelima's mother was never happy with anything that I did.

Neelima wanted me to come and live in the flat. There were three empty bedrooms, but her mother did not want me there. So I lived in a chawl in Ghatkopar and came to the flat every day. Salim lived with me in the same room.

Tragedy Queen

Neelima talked to me about film-making. One day she took me to her bedroom and opened a large cupboard. It was full of video cassettes.

'These are cassettes of all my films,' she told me. 'There are one hundred and fourteen.' She pointed to the first shelf. 'These are some of my earliest films. They are mostly comedies[32]. The more serious films are on the next two shelves.'

Then she pointed to the last four shelves. 'These are all tragedies. I was called the "Tragedy Queen". This is my favourite film.' She pointed to a cassette. 'It's *Mumtaz Mahal*. I played the role[33] of the Emperor's wife.'

'Was it your greatest role?' I asked.

She smiled sadly. 'It was a wonderful role, yes,' she replied. 'But one day I shall play an even greater role.'

———

Something wonderful happened. Neelima's mother died. A month later, Neelima asked me to come and live in the flat. But she kindly continued to pay for Salim's room in the chawl.

Neelima began to go out more often. Sometimes she did not return at night. I was sure that she had a lover. Perhaps she would get married soon.

One evening she said to me, 'Ram, I want you to stay at the chawl tomorrow. Just for one night.'

'Why, Madam?' I asked.

'Don't ask questions,' she said. 'Just do it.'

She told me to do this three times in the next three months. I felt sure that her lover visited her when I was away. One morning, I left the chawl very early and went back to Neelima's flat. At six o'clock the door opened and a man came out. He was tall, and he was wearing blue jeans and a white shirt. He had some money in one hand and some car keys in the other. I knew his face. Where had I seen him? I could not remember exactly.

I went into the flat at seven o'clock as usual. Then I saw

I knew his face. Where had I seen him?

Neelima, and I was shocked. There were bruises[34] all over her face, and she had a black eye.

'Madam!' I cried. 'What has happened to you?'

'It is nothing to worry about, Ram,' she said. 'I fell from my bed and hurt myself.'

I did not believe her. I knew that the man I saw leaving the flat had done this to her.

After that day, Neelima became strangely quiet. One morning I saw her with a black eye again.

'Who is doing this to you?' I asked her.

She was quiet for a moment, then she said, 'There is a man in my life, Ram. Sometimes I think that he loves me. Sometimes I think that he hates me.'

'Why don't you leave him?' I asked.

'It is not that easy,' she said.

———

Her lover had visited her again. She was lying in bed with a long, deep cut under her left eye and her face was bruised. She had difficulty speaking.

'We must call the police, Madam,' I said. 'He must be arrested.'

'No, Ram,' she said. 'I'll be all right. That man is never going to come here again.'

But after that, she became even more quiet. She sent her cook and maid away, and I was the only one working in the flat. And then Neelima prepared for the greatest role of her life.

She asked me to get all her awards and the film magazines with her picture on the front. She put on her most expensive sari and jewellery and made her face look absolutely beautiful. Then she went into her bedroom and put the video cassette of her film *Mumtaz Mahal* into the video recorder. She pushed 'Play' and sat down on the bed. The film began. She told me to go shopping.

Tragedy Queen

When I returned that evening, I found her on the bed. She was holding one of her awards. I took it from her and looked at it. I read: *National Award for Best Actress. Awarded to Neelima Kumari for her role in* Mumtaz Mahal, *1985.*

I looked at Neelima's dead body. I would not go to the police. I was afraid that they would arrest me for murder. So I ran away to the chawl in Ghatkopar.

'Why have you come here?' Salim asked me.

'Madam has sent me away,' I said.

'What will we do?' said Salim. 'How will we pay the rent for this room?'

'Don't worry,' I said. 'Neelima paid the rent for the next two months. By then I'm sure I'll have a new job.'

———

I got a job in a foundry[35]. Every day I was afraid the police would come to arrest me. But there was no news in the papers about Neelima Kumari's death.

Her body was discovered after a month. The newspapers said: *Famous Tragedy Queen, Neelima Kumari, kills herself.*

Now this was a real tragedy.

———

Smita is shaking her head sadly. 'How terrible,' she says. 'I've seen *Mumtaz Mahal.*'

'Are we going to talk about Neelima Kumari,' I say. 'Or shall I tell you about the quiz show?'

Smita presses 'Play' on the DVD player.

———

'OK, Mr Thomas,' said Prem Kumar. 'Here is the question for ten thousand rupees. In which year did Neelima Kumari, the Tragedy Queen, win the National Award for Best Actress? Was it a) 1984, b) 1988, c) 1986 or d) 1985?'

'I know the answer,' I said. 'It is D, 1985.'

'What?' Prem Kumar was so shocked that he forgot to ask if I was absolutely sure of my answer.

There was the sound of drums. The correct answer lit up on the screen.

'Absolutely correct!' said Prem Kumar. 'You have won ten thousand rupees.'

5
A Soldier's Story

We heard the air raid[36] warning siren[37] at eight-thirty, and everyone in the chawl hurried to the large basement under the school building. The Gokhales, the Nenes, the Bapats, Mr Wagle, Mr Kulkarni, Mrs Damle, Mr Shirke and Mrs Barwe. There were a few chairs, a table and a small television in the basement. It was hot, but we felt safe there.

It was the third night of the war. The women sat and talked, but the men listened carefully to the news. We children ran around the room shouting and playing war games. We also talked about the war.

'It's very exciting,' I said. 'My employer has given me a week's holiday because of the war.'

'Yes,' said Putul. 'And my school is closed for a week.'

'I wish that we could have a war every month,' said Dhyanesh.

'Don't be stupid!' someone shouted at us. We turned and saw an old man. He was tall and thin and had only one leg. 'War is very serious,' he said. 'People are killed in wars.'

We learnt that the man's name was Balwant Singh and that he was an old soldier.

'Which war did you fight in?' Mr Wagle asked him.

'The war in 1971,' said Mr Singh. 'The last *real* war. Do you want to hear my story?'

We all sat around the old soldier and Mr Wagle turned off the television.

Balwant Singh started speaking with a dreamy, faraway look in his eyes. 'It began on the third of December, 1971,' he said. 'On the same day, my wife wrote to tell me that our first child

32

A Soldier's Story

had been born. A boy. "*I will pray for your safety*," she wrote.

'That night, Pakistan carried out air attacks on several of our airfields[38]. Then soldiers began attacking us in Chhamb, a village in the north. I was in Chhamb with my regiment[39]. I was in a bunker[40] with three men – Sukhvinder Singh, Rajeshwar and Karnail Singh. Karnail was the best. He was not afraid of dying, but he was afraid of being buried. When the Pakistanis found dead Indian soldiers, they did not return them to us. They buried their bodies in the Muslim manner, and did not cremate[41] them like Hindus.

'"Sir," Karnail said to me. "If I die, promise me that you'll see that I'm cremated."

'"You are not going to die," I told him. But he made me promise.

'So on the night of the third of December, the enemy started shooting rockets[42] at us. We began moving forward quietly, in a straight line. Suddenly, a rocket exploded[43] behind us, killing Sukhvinder and Rajeshwar. Karnail had a wound[44] in his stomach, but I was only slightly hurt. I quickly spoke to my commander on the radio and told him what had happened.

'"The enemy are launching[45] rockets from a bunker, Sir," I said.

'"I cannot send anyone to help you, Balwant," he said. "But try to destroy the rocket launcher."

'"I'm going towards the enemy bunker," I told Karnail.

'"But you'll be killed, Sir!" he said. "Let me do it. You have a wife and a son. I have no one. But don't forget your promise." And before I could speak, he pulled the gun from my hand and ran forward. "Long Live Mother India!" he cried.'

'What happened to him?' asked Mr Wagle.

'He killed the three enemy soldiers with the rocket launcher. But then he, too, was shot dead,' said Balwant Singh. 'I did not move for nearly two hours. Karnail's body was lying near the enemy bunker, and I was thinking about my promise. But how

A Soldier's Story

many Pakistani soldiers were still around? I did not know.

'By three o'clock in the morning, the guns had stopped and everything was quiet. At last, I moved slowly towards the enemy bunker. It was about sixty or seventy metres away. Suddenly, in front of me, I heard the sound of footsteps. They came nearer and nearer. Then I saw a light as a Pakistani soldier lit a cigarette. He was no more than three metres away from me!

'I ran forward and he turned round. Then he saw my gun and dropped his. "Please don't kill me!" he cried.

'"How many of you are still near here?" I asked him.

'"I don't know," he said. "I'm lost, and I'm trying to find my way back. Please don't kill me!"

'"You are the enemy," I told him.

'"But I am also an ordinary man, like you," he said. "I have a wife and a baby girl. My daughter was born ten days ago, and I don't want to die without even seeing her face."

'"I also have a wife and a new baby son," I said. "But what would you have done to me?"

'"I would have killed you," he said after a moment.

'I nodded. "We are soldiers," I said. "We have to kill the enemy. But I promise to have you buried." Then I killed him silently with my bayonet[46].'

Mrs Damle closed her eyes. 'Terrible, terrible!' she said.

'War *is* terrible,' said Balwant Singh.

'What happened next?' asked Mr Wagle.

'I carried Karnail's body back to my commander,' said Balwant Singh. 'The next morning, we cremated Karnail. He was awarded an MVC.'

'What's an MVC?' asked Dhyanesh.

'Maha Vir Chakra,' said Balwant Singh. 'It's one of the highest awards for bravery given in the Indian armed forces[47]. The highest is the PVC or Param Vir Chakra.'

'What award did you get?' asked Dhyanesh.

'I did not get an award,' said the old soldier. 'But it's not the end of my story. I must tell you about Mandiala Bridge.'

Mr Wagle looked at his watch. 'We've had enough excitement for one night,' he said. 'And it's past midnight, so we can return to our houses.'

The next day, we were in the bunker again. On the television, some men were discussing the war. Mr Kulkarni turned it off.

'Let's listen instead to our war hero,' he said. He turned to Balwant Singh. 'Tell us about Mandiala Bridge.'

Balwant looked pleased. 'We knew that the Pakistanis' plan was to capture Mandiala Bridge,' he explained. 'If that happened, we would have to leave Chhamb and the places west of Tawi.

'At three o'clock on the morning of the fifth of December, they attacked. There were Pakistani tanks[48] shooting at us on the ground, and Pakistani planes dropping bombs[49] on us from above. Our commander was killed and many of our soldiers were shot. The next morning, the enemy's flag was flying above Mandiala Bridge.

'Then the commander of 368 Brigade arrived from Akhnoor. He looked around and saw dead bodies everywhere. Those soldiers that were still alive were running away.

'"Balwant Singh," he said to me. "What is happening? Where are all our men going?"

'"They are running away," I told him. "But I will fight until the end, Sir."

'"Good man, Balwant," he said.

'When the fighting started again, Mandiala Bridge was filled with fires and explosions. Bullets[50] went past us, enemy planes flew over our heads and bombs exploded all around us. But we ran forward and attacked our enemy, shooting and killing many men. Then the Pakistanis decided to bring their tanks across the Tawi river.

A Soldier's Story

'"We must stop them crossing the bridge," the commander said.

'But when the Pakistani tanks began coming across the bridge, two of our men left their tanks and ran away. I immediately jumped into one of our empty tanks and began driving it towards the Pakistani bunker. They continued to fire at me, but I did not stop. After twenty minutes only one Pakistani tank was left. I chased it when it tried to get away. My tank was hit by an enemy shot and caught fire, but I continued to chase the last tank. Suddenly, that tank exploded.

'All the enemy tanks were now destroyed,' Balwant Singh went on. 'But there were some rocket launchers around the bridge, and the Pakistani flag was still flying above it. *I had to pull it down*. I began moving towards the Pakistani bunker. When I was ten metres from the bunker, I started shooting. Three of the four soldiers in the bunker died. I was going to shoot the fourth when I realized I had no more bullets. The Pakistani soldier saw this and smiled. He shot at me, and several bullets hit my left leg. I fell to the ground and he pointed his gun at my chest. I said my prayers and was ready to die. But when he tried to fire, there was only a CLICK! His gun was also empty! He shouted and ran towards me, but I stood up quickly and hit him on the head – hard! He fell to the ground and did not move.

'Finally, I pulled down the enemy's flag and replaced it with the Indian flag. It was the happiest moment of my life.'

Balwant Singh stopped speaking, and we saw that his eyes were filled with tears. Nobody moved for almost a minute. Then Dhyanesh asked the same question again.

'So which award did they give you for this?' he said.

'They didn't give me anything,' Balwant said after a moment.

Everyone was silent again. Suddenly, all the children started to walk past Balwant Singh, shaking hands with this brave soldier.

I immediately jumped into one of the empty tanks and began driving it towards the Pakistani bunker.

A Soldier's Story

Balwant Singh cried tears of happiness, then he hurried out of the room on his one leg.

———

The next day, a man came to collect money for a soldiers' charity. He told us that our soldiers were doing a great job. Our country was great. Our prime minister was great. We were great. And the money that we gave, he said, should also be great. He passed round a box, and people put money in it.

Balwant Singh was not there. He was not feeling well.

'Did you fight in the 1971 war?' Mr Kulkarni asked the man from the charity.

'Yes, of course,' the man said. 'I was in Chhamb.'

'Did you get any awards?' asked Kulkarni.

'Yes,' he said. 'I was a commander at Mandiala Bridge.'

'What kind of person are you?' said Kulkarni. 'You take awards yourself, but do not give them to the man who won back the bridge from the enemy's army.'

'I don't understand,' said the man. 'Who are you talking about?'

'Our own soldier,' said Kulkarni. 'He was a hero during the 1971 war.' Then he told him Balwant Singh's story.

'Where is this great soldier?' the man asked.

We took the man to Balwant Singh's room and waited outside while they talked. Soon we heard loud voices arguing, then the man came out. He was very angry.

'That man is not a war hero!' he shouted at us. 'He ran away from Chhamb! He should be in prison! Everything that he told you was a lie. Let me tell you his true story.

'Balwant Singh's first child had just been born when the war started,' the man explained. 'He wanted to be with his family so he ran away from the fighting. He managed to reach his house in Pathankot and hid there. Two days after he arrived, a Pakistani bomb fell on his house, killing his wife and son. But Balwant only lost a leg.'

A Soldier's Story

The man from the soldiers' charity finished speaking and we did not know what to say. After a few minutes, the man left, still very angry.

Balwant Singh did not come out of his room that evening.

When Mr Kulkarni went to look for him the next morning, he found only an empty room. Balwant Singh had left the chawl.

Smita is looking serious.

'Where were you during the war?' I ask her.

'I was here, in Mumbai,' she replies, then goes on quickly. 'Let's see the next question.'

'Are you ready for the next question for fifty thousand rupees, Mr Thomas?' said Prem Kumar.

'I'm ready,' I replied.

'What is the highest award given to the Indian armed forces?' he asked. 'Is it a) Maha Vir Chakra, b) Param Vir Chakra, c) Shaurya Chakra or d) Ashok Chakra?'

I knew that the audience did not believe I could answer this question. They looked at me with sympathy[51] and I could see that they were ready to say goodbye to this poor waiter.

'B. Param Vir Chakra,' I replied.

'Are you absolutely sure?' said Prem Kumar, looking shocked. 'Or are you just guessing?'

'I am sure,' I said.

There was the sound of drums. The correct answer lit up on the screen.

'Absolutely correct!' said Prem Kumar. 'You have won fifty thousand rupees.'

6
A Brother's Promise

One morning, I heard strange voices in the chawl. New neighbours were moving into the room next door.

'Thomas!' I heard a voice I knew. It was Mr Ramakrishna. Mr Ramakrishna was the chawl's manager. He was the man we had to beg when we had no money to pay the rent. He also looked after the building. We had asked him several times to repair part of the first-floor wooden railing[52] which had become weak and dangerous, but he still hadn't done it.

I came out of our room and saw him with a short man who was about fifty years old.

'Thomas, this is Mr Shantaram,' said Mr Ramakrishna. 'He's going to live in the room next to yours with his wife and daughter.'

I looked past them into Shantaram's room. His daughter was older than me, with long black hair. She was sitting on the bed. His wife had grey hair. Shantaram saw me looking at them and quickly shut the door so that I could not see them.

'What do you do?' I asked him.

'I'm really an astronomer[53],' he explained. 'But at the moment I'm managing a shop. We won't be staying here long. We'll be moving to a very nice apartment in Nariman Point very soon.'

I knew that Mr Shantaram was lying. People who could afford to live in Nariman Point never lived in chawls.

―――――

The walls of the rooms inside the chawl were very thin. When you put a cup or glass against the wall and put your ear against it, you could listen to everything happening in the next room. Salim and I often did this with our neighbours.

A Brother's Promise

One night I put a cup against the wall and I could hear Mr Shantaram speaking.

'I don't deserve to be here,' he was saying. 'There are two street boys living next to us. Gudiya, do not speak to any boy in the chawl or I'll hit you. Do you understand?'

I was so shocked that I dropped the cup.

Over the next two weeks, I only saw Mr Shantaram two or three times. I never saw his wife or daughter. When I returned home from work, they would stay inside the room.

It was nine o'clock at night. Salim was looking at a film magazine. I had my cup against the wall and I could hear Shantaram speaking to his daughter.

'Look through the telescope,' he was telling her. 'Can you see the bright-red thing in the sky? That is Mars.'

'Quick, get a cup,' I told Salim. 'You must hear this.'

Salim also put a cup to the wall. For the next thirty minutes, we heard all about the stars and the planets of the night sky. It was wonderful.

A week later, a new sound came from Shantaram's room. 'Meow!' I hurried to the wall with my cup.

Gudiya was speaking. 'Papa, look, I found a cat. Can I keep him? He is so small.'

'OK,' said Shantaram. 'You should call him Pluto, it's the smallest planet.'

Perhaps Shantaram is not so bad, I told myself.

Then, one evening, we did not need our cups to hear him shouting at his wife and daughter. He threw books at the wall, then started breaking cups and plates.

Salim and I were very frightened and we could only relax when Shantaram had gone to sleep.

The next night we heard a lot of screaming. I ran outside.

A Brother's Promise

Mrs Shantaram asked me to get a taxi to take Gudiya to the hospital.

Two days later, Mrs Shantaram asked me to visit Gudiya. 'She feels very lonely,' she said. 'Perhaps you can talk to her.'

So I went with Mrs Shantaram to the hospital. On the way, she told me what had happened. Shantaram had thrown a boiling cup of tea at his wife. Gudiya had tried to get in front of her mother, but the tea had burnt her face.

Gudiya's face was covered with bandages[54]. I could only see her eyes.

'Look, Ram Mohammad Thomas has come to see you, Gudiya,' Mrs Shantaram said.

I relaxed when I saw Gudiya's eyes smiling up at me. I knew she was pleased to see me. I sat with her for three hours and we talked about different things. I told her about my work at the foundry, and she told me that she would soon start studying at university.

Mrs Shantaram tried to explain her husband's behaviour. 'He is a famous space scientist,' she told me. 'Or he *was* a space scientist at the Space Research Institute. He studied stars through a big telescope, and three years ago he discovered a new star. It was a very important discovery. But then another astronomer said that *he* had discovered it. After that, my husband became very upset. Then he started fighting with people at the Institute. They made him leave, and since then he has been doing any job that he can find.'

'Can I do anything to help you?' I asked Gudiya.

'Please look after Pluto until I return home,' she said.

'Yes, of course,' I said.

She put her hand on my hand. 'You are like a brother to me,' she said.

I did not know what to say, but I held on to Gudiya's hand very tightly.

A Brother's Promise

'I like Gudiya very much,' I told Salim. 'I have to stop Shantaram from hurting her.'

'What can you do?' said Salim. 'It's his family. And remember, it is not a good idea to interfere[55] in other people's lives.'

I had no answer to that.

———

Gudiya came home from hospital, but I did not see her. A week later I heard her crying and I knew that I had to do something. A brother had to help his sister.

Unfortunately there was a wall between us. But there was a small hole at the bottom of the wall. It was big enough for me to put my hand through.

'Sister, don't cry,' I called to her. 'Hold my hand.'

And someone did hold my hand. Immediately a feeling of deep love passed through me. I became part of Gudiya and could feel her pain as if it was my own.

Salim was watching me. 'Are you crazy?' he said.

———

The next night, Shantaram came home angry again and began to shout and scream at his wife and daughter. When I heard Gudiya cry out in pain, I ran to Mr Ramakrishna's room.

'Mr Shantaram is beating his wife and daughter,' I said.

'We cannot interfere,' he told me. 'Go away, it's time for my sleep.'

I ran back to my room. Shantaram was sleeping now, and I put my hand through the hole in the wall. Gudiya held it.

'When he hits me, I want to die,' she said.

'He will never hurt you again,' I said. 'That is a brother's promise.'

———

The next evening, Shantaram returned from work and climbed the stairs to the first floor. When Shantaram was next to the weak wooden railing, I ran at him from behind. I pushed him

When Shantaram was next to the weak wooden railing, I ran at him from behind.

A Brother's Promise

against the railing – and it broke. Shantaram fell to the ground below. He landed face-down and did not move.

Suddenly, I realized what I had done. I had killed him! The police would arrest me and hang[56] me for this!

I did not wait another moment. I did not say goodbye to my best friend, Salim, or to my new sister, Gudiya. I ran down the stairs and out of the building. I ran to the train station and got on a train. I was going to the only other city that I knew. Delhi.

Smita is silent while I am telling her this story. There are tears in her eyes. Perhaps this is because she is a woman and can imagine Gudiya's pain.

'Let's see the next question,' I say.

I press 'Play' on the DVD player.

'Our next question for one hundred thousand rupees is from the world of astronomy,' Prem Kumar was saying. 'Which is the smallest planet? Is it a) Pluto, b) Mars, c) Neptune or d) Mercury?'

'A,' I told him.

'A?' he said.

'Yes, the answer is A. Pluto,' I said.

'Are you absolutely sure of your answer?'

'Yes,' I said.

There was the sound of drums. The correct answer lit up on the screen.

'Absolutely correct!' said Prem Kumar. 'Mr Thomas, you have won one hundred thousand rupees.'

7
How to Speak Australian

Colonel Taylor was forty-six and he was a diplomat for the Australian government. His wife, Rebecca, was forty-four. Their son, Roy, was fifteen, and their daughter, Maggie, was seventeen. Maggie was very beautiful, with blue eyes and fair hair.

The Taylors had been very kind to me. Not many people would employ someone who just arrived at their house one day from Mumbai. I was lucky. They needed a servant quickly because they had just sacked[57] the last one.

In the fifteen months that I had been with the family, five more servants had been sacked from their jobs. This was because Colonel Taylor was 'The Man Who Knows'.

Jagdish, the gardener, stole plants from the garden and Colonel Taylor knew. Jagdish was sacked the next day. Sheela, the maid, took a bracelet from Mrs Taylor's room and Colonel Taylor knew. Sheela was sacked. Raju, the cook, drank some of the Colonel's whisky. He was sacked. Ajay, the new cook, planned to steal some money and told his plan to a friend on the phone. He was sacked the next day, and he and his friend were arrested by the police. Basanti, the new maid, put on one of Maggie's dresses. She was sacked the next day.

How did Colonel Taylor know about things that happened behind closed doors, in the middle of the night or on the telephone? It was very mysterious. None of us could understand it.

Only Shanti, the new maid, and I could go into the family's private rooms. But we could not go into the Colonel's office – he called it The Den[58]. The Den was a small room next to his bedroom. It had a heavy wooden door with three locks. Only the Colonel could go in there. Not even Mrs Taylor, Roy or Maggie were allowed in.

My time with the Taylors had helped me to forget the things that had happened in Mumbai. Shantaram and Neelima Kumari were now almost forgotten. I sometimes thought about Gudiya. And I could not forget Salim. I felt guilty about leaving him behind, but I was afraid to write to him or phone him.

Living with the Taylors, I had learnt to like a lot of Australian things. But I found it difficult to *speak* like an Australian. Every evening in my room, I practised. 'G'*day Maite, see you at aight at India Gaite,*' and then I would laugh at myself.

Roy and Maggie received a magazine every month. It was called *Australian Geographic*. It was full of pictures of wonderful places in Australia.

I did not have much work to do. Ramu was the cook and he looked after the kitchen. Shanti made the beds and washed the clothes. I did the cleaning and sometimes I helped Bhagwati, the new gardener, in the garden.

The servants had three rooms. One was large and the other two were small. Bhagwati lived in the large room with his wife and son. Shanti lived in the second room. Ramu and I shared the third room.

Ramu was a nice man and a very good cook. Shanti liked him very much, but Ramu was in love with someone else. Her name was a secret, but I can tell you that she was a very beautiful girl with blue eyes and fair hair.

Colonel Taylor did not give me all of my salary. He paid me fifty rupees each month and promised to give me the rest of my money when my employment with him ended. I had one hundred rupees in my pocket, but 'the rest' of my salary now totalled 22,500 rupees.

Every night I dreamt of visiting the places that I had seen in *Australian Geographic*. I bought thirty of these magazines from the man who collected all the old magazines and newspapers that the Taylors did not want.

It was past midnight and Ramu was not asleep.

'What's the matter, Ramu?' I asked.

'How can I sleep, Thomas?' he said. 'I am thinking about my beautiful girl.'

'You are stupid,' I told him. 'If Colonel Taylor finds out, he'll sack you.'

Ramu smiled and put something into my hand. It was a photograph of Maggie.

'My God!' I cried. 'Where did you get this?'

'I took it from her room,' Ramu explained. 'You must not tell anyone, Thomas. Promise me.'

Two days later, a police car arrived. The policemen pulled Ramu from the kitchen and took him to our room. They searched the room and found money and a diamond necklace in his bed. They found my *Australian Geographic* magazines in one corner of the room. And then they found the photograph of Maggie in *my* bed! How did it get there? I did not know.

I was taken to the Taylors like a thief.

'You only mentioned one thief in the house, Colonel Taylor,' said the police inspector. 'And we found the diamond necklace and a lot of stolen money in his bed. But look at these magazines!' He dropped them on the floor, then pointed at me. 'And we also found this.' The inspector held out the photograph of Maggie.

Maggie began crying. Ramu looked sick. Colonel Taylor looked angrier than I had ever seen him before.

'You too, Thomas?' shouted Mrs Taylor. 'You Indians! We feed you, and what do you do? You steal from us.'

'No, Rebecca,' Colonel Taylor told his wife. 'Thomas did not steal these things. Ramu hid the photograph in Thomas's bed. *I know.*'

Again, Colonel Taylor was The Man Who Knows.

I got my *Australian Geographic* magazines back. Ramu said that, yes, he had taken the photograph from Maggie's room, but he had not stolen the necklace. He said that it was Shanti. But the policemen only took Ramu away in the police car.

―――

The Taylors got a dog for Maggie and she decided to call him Rover. A new cook was employed. His name was Jai. I did not like him.

'I want to open a garage, but it will cost a lot of money,' he told me one day. 'How much money do these people have in the house? Do you know?'

I did not answer.

―――

Colonel Taylor started to go on early-morning walks with Rover. He went to Lodhi Gardens, near the house. I was ordered to go with him to clean up after Rover. Sometimes on these walks, Colonel Taylor disappeared for several minutes. I thought that it was strange, so one morning I decided to follow him. I saw him talking to a man who I knew was from the Ministry of Defence[59]. I had seen this man before, at parties at the house.

'I followed you last night from your house in South Ex to the sweet shop, Mr Kumar,' said the Colonel. 'You must be more careful.'

'I'm very sorry, Colonel, Sir,' said Jeevan Kumar. 'I know that people must not see us together. Meet me on Friday the fourteenth in the car park behind Balsons in South Ex. At eight pm. OK?'

'OK,' said Colonel Taylor.

I hurried back to Rover before Colonel Taylor returned.

―――

On Friday the fourteenth, Colonel Taylor said to his wife, 'I shall be late for dinner tonight, Rebecca. Don't wait for me.'

Why did the Colonel lie to his wife about his meeting? Suddenly, I did not like him as much as before, and I felt sorry for Mrs Taylor.

Colonel Taylor's mother had died in Australia, in Adelaide. Everyone was very sad.

'We are all going to be away for a week,' Colonel Taylor told Jai. 'The house will be locked. You, Thomas and the others can eat outside.'

But that night, Jai broke into[60] the Taylors' house and went to The Den. He broke the locks and pushed open the heavy wooden door.

I woke up to the sound of someone shouting inside the Taylors' house. I ran into the house and discovered Jai in The Den.

'There is not one rupee in this house!' he screamed angrily.

'Jai, what have you done?' I shouted.

'I thought that Colonel Taylor had money and jewels in this room, but there is nothing.' He looked at me. 'I'm taking one of the video recorders and a TV, and I'm leaving. Don't call the police or I'll break every bone in your body.'

After Jai had gone, I looked around the room. It was full of strange things. Tiny cameras, books about spying[61] and papers with the word SECRET written on them.

Then I saw a box full of video tapes with names on them: Ajay, Bhagwati, High Commissioner, Jeevan, Jones, Maggie, McGill, Raj, Ramesh, Rebecca, Roy, Shanti, Stuart. And Thomas.

I found a video recorder in a cupboard. I put my tape into it and pushed 'Play'.

Moments later, I saw myself moving around my room. Now I knew how the Colonel became The Man Who Knows. He had tiny cameras hidden all over the house! But I would say

Now I knew how the Colonel became The Man Who Knows.

nothing about this. I had saved 43,500 rupees of my salary, and I hoped to get it one day.

But I decided to telephone Colonel Taylor and tell him about Jai.

'What?' shouted Colonel Taylor. 'Listen, Thomas. Put a new lock on the door of The Den. Do not let anyone into the room and do not enter it yourself. And do not call the police. I will get a plane back to Delhi immediately.'

'Yes, Sir,' I said.

Colonel Taylor returned and ran straight to The Den. After a minute or two, he came out again. 'Thank God,' he said. 'Nothing has been taken. Well done, Thomas.'

———

I had been waiting near the phone all day. Maggie was waiting for a call from James, her new boyfriend. She had told me to pick up the phone before her father did in The Den.

The phone rang at seven-fifteen pm and I picked it up quickly. But not quickly enough. I heard the Colonel say 'Hello' from his phone in The Den.

After a moment, I heard Jeevan Kumar say, 'Meet me tomorrow, Thursday, at eight pm at the Ice Cream Shop near India Gate. I have exciting information.'

'Good,' said Colonel Taylor, and he put down the phone.

———

At ten pm the next night, a police car arrived at the house. The inspector who had arrested Ramu got out. The police chief and Colonel Taylor were with him. Some minutes later, the Australian high commissioner arrived.

'Why is Colonel Taylor now *persona non grata*?' he asked the police chief. 'Why must he leave the country in forty-eight hours?'

'We discovered him taking secret papers from a man called Jeevan Kumar,' said the police chief. 'Kumar works at the Ministry of Defence.'

How to Speak Australian

Colonel Taylor looked at the ground and said nothing.

The high commissioner looked sad. 'This is the first time any of my officers have been *persona non grata*,' he said. 'And believe me, Charles is not a spy. But I understand that he must leave the country. Tell me, how did you know about Charles' meeting with Kumar?'

'One of your Australians phoned me this morning, Sir,' said the inspector.

'How do you know that he was an Australian?' asked the high commissioner.

'Because he *spoke* like an Australian,' said the inspector. 'He said, "G'*day Maite, go to India Gaite, tonight at aight.*" Only an Australian speaks like that.'

―――

The next day, Colonel Taylor left Delhi. Mrs Taylor and the children would follow later. I was leaving the Taylors, too. I had thirty *Australian Geographic* magazines, which I would sell, and 52,000 rupees. I was going to meet Salim in Mumbai.

―――

Smita looks at her watch. It is one-thirty am.

'Do you want to go on?' I ask.

'We must,' she says. And she pushes the 'Play' button.

―――

'The next question for two hundred thousand rupees is about government diplomats,' said Prem Kumar. 'When a government says that a diplomat is *persona non grata*, what does it mean? Is it a) that the diplomat will get an award, b) that the diplomat is going to stay in the country for a longer time, c) that the diplomat is grateful or d) that the diplomat is not acceptable[62] and must leave? Do you understand the question, Mr Thomas?'

'Yes,' I replied. 'My answer is D. The diplomat is not acceptable and must leave.'

There were cries of surprise from the audience.

'Are you absolutely sure of your answer?'

'Yes,' I said.

There was the sound of drums. The correct answer lit up on the screen.

'Absolutely correct!' said Prem Kumar. 'You have won two hundred thousand rupees.' Then he turned to the audience and said, 'Tonight, Mr Thomas really is The Man Who Knows!'

8
Murder on a Train

Delhi's Paharganj railway station was busy with passengers. I was walking towards the Mumbai train, wearing a new white shirt and jeans. There was a porter walking next to me, carrying my suitcase on his head. I had paid him to carry it.

There were some *Australian Geographic* magazines, a few clothes and a game for Salim in my suitcase. But not my money. I had heard many stories about thieves on trains. They took your luggage when you were asleep. My fifty thousand rupees from the Taylors were inside my trousers. I had used the other two thousand rupees to pay for my clothes, my train ticket and the game for Salim.

I was in railway coach S7. It was almost at the end of the train. My sleeping berth[63] was next to the door, and I put my suitcase under it.

My cabin had six berths. One was above me, two were in front of me and two were on the side. A family of four were sitting on the lower berth opposite me. The boy was about twelve years old, the girl was a little older. Their father was a businessman and wore a black coat and cap. His wife wore a green sari. The boy was tall and looked friendly. His sister was the most beautiful girl I had ever seen.

The train left the station and, after a time, the boy came and sat next to me. His name was Akshay and his sister was Meenakshi. They lived in Delhi and were going to Mumbai for an uncle's wedding. Akshay was excited about his computer games. I told him that I spoke English, read *Australian Geographic* and had seven girlfriends. I told him that I had all the latest computer games and that I was going to Mumbai to meet my best friend, Salim.

Murder on a Train

Akshay did not believe me. 'You don't know anything about computers,' he said. 'You are just a big liar.'

This made me angry. 'Let me tell you, Mr Akshay, that I have fifty thousand rupees,' I said. 'Have you ever seen so much money?'

'Show me!' he said.

I pushed my hand inside my trousers and brought out an envelope. I took out the thousand-rupee notes and waved them under his nose, then quickly put them back in the envelope and back inside my trousers.

Akshay's eyes opened wide with surprise. I could see that he thought differently about me now. Suddenly, I was more important.

———

I was woken up by a man with a thick beard and a revolver[64] in his left hand. He wore a white shirt and black trousers and had long hair.

'This is a robbery,' he said calmly.

He was young and looked like a college student. But I had never seen a train robber before. Perhaps they all looked like college students.

'I want you all to climb down from your berths,' he said.

We all sat on the lower berths. Akshay and his father sat next to me. Meenakshi and her mother sat opposite us.

The robber had an open bag over his shoulder. 'I want the men to give me their watches and money, and the women to give me their jewellery,' he said. 'Do it, or I will shoot you.'

Meenakshi began to cry quietly. Her mother dropped her bracelet and necklace into the robber's bag, her father put in his watch and his money. I took out the last of the rupees in my shirt pocket and put them into the bag.

The robber looked happy and was about to leave when Akshay called out, 'Wait!' He pointed at me. 'This boy has got fifty thousand rupees!'

Murder on a Train

The robber stared angrily at Akshay. 'Is this some kind of joke?' he asked.

But Akshay shook his head. 'No,' he replied. 'The money's hidden in his trousers.'

Then the robber turned to me and put the gun in front of my face. 'Give it to me now!' he said.

I could not argue with a gun, so I took the envelope from inside my trousers and gave it to him. He opened it and smiled when he saw the money. Then he dropped it into his bag.

I was very angry. Fifty thousand dreams had suddenly been taken from me. Without thinking about it, I jumped on the robber. He was surprised, but he quickly pushed the revolver against my stomach. Just as he was about to shoot, I turned the revolver towards his chest. Then there was a loud BANG and a red stain[65] appeared on his white shirt.

'Oh, my God!' I heard Akshay cry.

Suddenly, the robber was lying on the floor and I had his gun in my hand. I stared at it. The revolver had the name COLT on it. People came from other parts of the railway coach to see what had happened. Men, women and children stared at the dead robber lying on the floor.

I thought about the police. Would they tell me that I was a hero for killing a robber? Or would they call me a killer who had shot a man dead without even knowing his name? I was not going to wait to find out.

Just as the train was about to stop at the next station, I jumped out of the door with the gun still in my hand. I did not have time to take my money from the robber's bag, I only cared about getting away. I ran and jumped on to another train which was just leaving the station. When it went over a bridge, I threw the revolver into a dark river.

I could not go to Mumbai. I was afraid that Akshay had told the police about Salim, and that they would find me and arrest me in Ghatkopar. At nine o'clock in the morning, the

I could not argue with a gun, so I took the envelope from inside my trousers and gave it to him.

Murder on a Train

train stopped at a busy, crowded railway station. A sign at the station said: AGRA. I got off the train.

―――

Smita puts her hand over her mouth. 'Oh, my God,' she says. 'All this time you have been living with the guilt of killing a man?'

'Two men,' I say. 'Don't forget Shantaram.'

'But the murder on the train was an accident,' she says.

'I know,' I say. 'Now let's look at the quiz show.'

―――

Prem Kumar turned to me. 'Are you ready? OK, here's the next question. It is about guns. Who invented the revolver? Was it a) Samuel Colt, b) Bruce Browning, c) Dan Wesson or d) James Revolver?'

I thought hard.

'Do you know any of these names?' Prem Kumar asked me.

'I know one of them,' I said.

'OK, so what is your answer?' he asked.

'A. Colt,' I said.

'Are you absolutely sure of your answer?' he asked.

'Yes,' I said.

There was the sound of drums. The correct answer lit up on the screen.

'Absolutely correct!' said Prem Kumar. 'You have won five hundred thousand rupees.'

I could not believe it. I had won back ten times more than I had lost on that train.

9
A Love Story

After two hours, I left Agra railway station and began to walk through the crowded streets. After a time, I came to a river. On the opposite side there was a large white building. It was the largest and most beautiful building I had ever seen.

'Excuse me,' I said to a man who was stood near me. 'What is that building?'

He looked at me strangely. 'Don't you know?' he said. 'It's the Taj Mahal.'

A walk of thirty minutes brought me to the entrance. A large white sign read: *Taj Mahal Entry Prices: Indians Rs. 20 Foreigners $20. Mondays Closed, Fridays Free.*

Today was Friday, the twelfth of June. It seemed that today was my lucky day.

The Taj Mahal was full of people, young and old, rich and poor, Indian and foreign. I saw a group of foreign tourists listening to a guide.

'I will tell you the history of the Taj Mahal,' he was saying. 'One day in the year 1607, Prince Khurram fell in love with a girl called Mumtaz. They were married in the year 1612, and over the next eighteen years they had fourteen children …'

He continued to speak for some time, then the group moved on. I was about to go with them when someone said, 'Excuse me, can you speak English?'

I turned round to see a man with his wife and two children staring at me.

'Yes,' I replied.

'Please can you tell us a little about the Taj Mahal?' he asked. 'We are tourists. From Japan. We are new to your city. We arrived today.'

A Love Story

I felt like telling him that I was also new to this city, but I liked his face. 'The Taj Mahal was built by Emperor Khurram for his wife Mumtaz, who he married in 1512,' I said. 'They had eighteen children in fourteen years.'

The Japanese man said, 'Eighteen children in only *fourteen* years?'

'Yes,' I said. 'Anyway, when the nineteenth child was born, Mumtaz died. But before she died, she asked the Emperor to build the Taj Mahal.'

I talked for five minutes. When I had finished, the Japanese man thanked me and he put something into my hand. When he moved away, I saw that it was a fifty-rupee note. For just five minutes work!

———

It was getting dark when I left the Taj Mahal. I had to find a place to stay, so I stopped a young boy in the street. He was about my age. 'Excuse me,' I said. The boy turned and looked at me with the kindest eyes I had ever seen. 'I am new to this city. Can you show me a place to stay?'

The boy nodded his head and said, 'Uzo Q Fiks X Ckka Lgxyz.'

'Sorry,' I said. 'I do not understand this language. I will ask someone else.'

'Ejop Bkggks Hz,' he said, and he began to pull me along the street. His face was friendly, so I went with him. Fifteen minutes later, we were in front of a large house.

'Swapna Palace' said the sign next to a big iron gate. The boy opened the gate and we went inside. The house had a big garden. My new friend took me to the door of the house and rang the doorbell. A maid opened the door. She was dark-haired and good-looking.

'Oh it's you, Shankar,' she said. 'You know that Madam does not like you to come to the house.'

Shankar pointed at me. 'Dz Izzaao X Nkkh,' he said.

A Love Story

The maid looked at me. 'So Shankar has brought you here to stay,' she said. 'I'll call Madam.'

Soon after, a woman who was about forty years old appeared at the door. She was wearing expensive clothes and a lot of gold jewellery. She had cold eyes and I did not like her.

'Who are you?' she asked me. 'Why have you come with Shankar?'

'My name is Raju Sharma,' I said. I was not going to use my real name in that city. Not after killing a man on a train. 'I am new to Agra and I am looking for somewhere to stay.'

She looked at me a little more kindly as soon as I spoke in English. 'We have an outhouse[66] with rooms, but it is full,' she said. 'If you can wait a week, we can find you a room. It costs four hundred rupees a month. Lajwanti can show you the outhouse.'

'Thank you, Madam,' I said. 'I will take the room and pay you four hundred rupees next week.'

'Perhaps you can stay with Shankar for a week,' she said.

The dark-haired maid, Lajwanti, took me to the outhouse. It had a courtyard with about thirty rooms around it. Shankar's room had just one bed and a tiny kitchen. The room I would get was four rooms away from Shankar's.

'Who is Shankar?' I asked. 'I met him by the Taj Mahal.'

'He is an orphan,' Lajwanti said. 'There is something wrong with his brain, and he can only speak strange words. He walks around the city all day, but Madam is very kind to him. Shankar does not have to pay rent for his room, and Madam gives him money to buy food.'

I was shocked. I thought that Shankar seemed like an intelligent boy with a speech problem. He did not seem mentally[67] disabled.

'Tell me about Madam,' I said.

'Her real name is Swapna Devi,' she said. 'She is one of the richest women in Agra.'

A Love Story

That evening, Shankar cooked food for me and told me to sleep on his bed. He slept on the hard stone floor. His kindness brought tears to my eyes.

———

I had to pay Madam four hundred rupees in seven days, so I quickly learnt to be a Taj Mahal guide. I listened carefully to the English-speaking guides and tried to remember as much as I could.

I moved to my own room after a week, but I had learnt a lot about Shankar in those seven days. His strange-sounding words were not meaningless to him. He could also draw people beautifully, and he often dreamt of his mother. On two nights I heard him cry out, 'Mummy, Mummy' in his sleep. And I knew then that he had the ability to speak normally.

———

I met a girl! Her name was Nita. She was dark and beautiful and had white flowers in her long black hair. We met at the Taj Mahal. Although Nita had lived in Agra for many years, it was her first visit to the Taj. She did not have the money to pay for a guide, but I quickly offered to show her around anyway.

The next day, I saw her again. She smiled at me.

'Today I have money to pay you,' she said shyly.

I laughed. 'Do you want me to take you round again?'

Nita looked at the ground. 'Yes, please,' she said.

So we walked and I began to give her the same information that I had given her the day before. But I soon realized that she was not really listening. She just wanted to be with me!

Nita came to the Taj most days after that. We sat and talked and I knew that I was falling in love with her. But when I told her this, she did not answer.

'Is something wrong?' I asked.

She did not answer. 'I have to go,' she said after a moment. And she hurried away.

I did not understand. Did Nita have a secret?

A Love Story

Shankar came into my room. He was crying.

'What's the matter?' I asked. He pointed to a cut on his leg. 'Did you fall down?'

Shankar shook his head. He took me out into the courtyard and pointed to a small wall in the corner. The children from the outhouse were always jumping over it.

I nodded. I decided that he had jumped down from the wall and hurt his leg.

I did not see the mad street dog just below the wall.

It was a new year, and it brought new hopes and new dreams. Nita and I were both eighteen – we could get married. It was Friday evening and we were at the Taj Mahal. There was a full moon in the sky. We held hands and I looked at the Taj Mahal and then at Nita. She was even more beautiful than that amazing building.

'Do you love me?' I asked her.

'Yes,' she replied.

'Will you marry me?' I asked.

She was silent for some minutes, then she said, 'I can't marry you. I am engaged[68] to another man.'

Another man! Engaged! I could not believe it.

'Do you have to marry him?' I asked.

'Yes,' she said. 'He is rich and successful. He will pay my family forty thousand rupees if I marry him.'

'Perhaps I could pay them the money instead,' I said.

'Do you have forty thousand rupees?' asked Nita.

I had saved up only 480 rupees. 'I need another 39,520 rupees,' I told Nita, sadly. 'But we could run away.'

'No,' said Nita. 'My sister ran away with a man last year. My family found her, broke the man's legs and gave her no food for ten days.'

So we did not run away.

She was even more beautiful than that amazing building.

A Love Story

Shankar came into my room coughing and fell down on the bed. He looked tired and had pains in his arms and legs. 'Q Xh Oqyf,' he said.

By the next day, Shankar was very ill and I paid for a doctor to come. He looked at Shankar, then asked 'Has he had any cuts? Has he been bitten by a dog?'

I told him about Shankar's cut leg. He nodded his head, then he said Shankar had got rabies[69] and that he would die.

'Is there nothing that we can do?' I said.

'Have you got forty thousand rupees?' asked the doctor. 'That is the cost of the treatment for rabies.'

Everyone needed forty thousand rupees! And I had only four hundred.

I decided that Shankar could not stay on his own, so I took him to my room and gave him my bed. I slept on the ground. Later that night, I heard Shankar talking in his sleep.

'Mummy, Mummy!' he cried. 'I am sorry. Don't hit me! Don't hit me! I love you, Mummy. I draw pictures of you in my blue notebook.'

The next morning, I remembered the blue notebook and searched for it in Shankar's room. It was hidden under his bed and was full of pictures that he had drawn of a woman.

The woman was Swapna Devi.

'Swapna Devi is your mother,' I told Shankar, waving the blue notebook in front of him.

He was suddenly afraid and tried to take the book from me. 'Cqrz Hz Wxyf Hu Aqnya,' he said.

'I know that it is true, Shankar,' I said. 'She hit you and threw you out of the house. Is that why you cannot speak properly?'

'Ik Ik Ik Lgzxoz Akip Hjhhu,' he cried, but I had already left.

'Yes, why have you come to see me?' Madam asked me, some minutes later.

'I know your secret, Swapna Devi,' I told her. 'You are Shankar's mother.'

'It's a lie!' she screamed. 'Get out!'

'I want forty thousand rupees for Shankar's treatment,' I said. 'He has got rabies. You must give me the money or he will die in the next twenty-four hours.'

She looked at me for a moment, then she said, 'Perhaps death will be the best thing for him.'

It was the most terrible thing that I have ever heard a mother say.

―――――

That night, there was a party at the house. Many important people had come and I could hear them laughing and drinking. In my room, Shankar was dying.

At twelve forty-seven am, Shankar held my hand and cried 'Mummy, Mummy!' And then he died.

―――――

I was angry. I wanted to scream and shout. Instead, I picked up Shankar's body and carried him to the house. I walked straight through to the dining room. All the guests were sitting at the table, about to eat their dessert. I climbed on to the table and put Shankar's body down on it. Swapna Devi opened her mouth, but no words came out.

'Mrs Swapna Devi,' I said. 'Your son Kunwar Shankar Singh Gautam died half an hour ago. You did not pay for his treatment. Please pay for his funeral.'

Then I nodded at the guests and walked out into the night.

―――――

For the next two weeks, I did not go to the Taj Mahal and I did not see Nita. Then one of the people at the outhouse came to me with some news.

A Love Story

'There was a phone call,' he said. 'Someone called Nita phoned. She wants you to go to the Emergency Ward at Singhania Hospital.'

I ran all the way to the hospital. As I was running towards its entrance, I passed a man who I recognized. He was the same man that I had once seen leaving Neelima Kumari's apartment in Mumbai.

I carried on running until I entered the Emergency Ward.

'Where is Nita?' I asked a doctor.

'I am here, Raju.' Nita's voice was weak.

I saw her lying on a bed and I was shocked. There were bruises all over her face and there was blood on her teeth. She had a long, deep cut under her left eye.

I had seen injuries like these before.

'Who ... who did this to you?' I asked.

'The man I am to marry,' she said. 'I tried to tell him that I did not want to marry him – that I wanted to marry you. And he did this.'

At that moment, a man came into the room.

'This is my father,' Nita said. 'Father, this is Raju. He ...'

'*You!*' Nita's father shouted at me. 'How dare[70] you come here! This has happened to Nita because of you!'

'That's not true,' I said.

'It is true!' he shouted. 'You are trying to take her away from the man that she is to marry. Have you offered to pay us forty thousand rupees? No.'

I wanted to kill the man, but I remembered that he was Nita's father. 'I will get the money,' I said suddenly. And I ran from the room and the hospital.

―――

I waited until Swapna Devi was not at home. When she left in her car to go to a party in the town, I climbed through her bedroom window. Lajwanti had once told me about Madam's safe[71] behind the picture in her bedroom. I discovered the

A Love Story

picture on the left wall of the room. It was a brightly-coloured picture of horses by someone called Husain.

I quickly took the picture from the wall and saw the safe behind it. Lajwanti had also said that Madam kept the key under her bed and it took me only a moment to find it.

I unlocked the safe and looked inside – and I got a surprise. It was nearly empty. There were no jewels, just some money, papers and a small photograph of a young child. The child was Shankar.

I took the money from the safe, locked it again and put the key back under the bed. Then I climbed out of the bedroom window and ran back to the outhouse.

I locked the door of my room and counted the money. There were 39,844 rupees. I found just 156 rupees in my pocket. But that made the forty thousand rupees that I needed.

I put the money in a paper bag and ran to the hospital. As I was entering the Emergency Ward, a man walked into me. He was wearing glasses and had thick black hair. I fell to the floor and dropped the bag from my hand. And the money fell out of it. The man picked up the money like an excited child. I thought that he was going to steal it, but he gave it back to me.

'This money is yours,' he said. 'But please lend it to me and save my son's life. He is only sixteen. He was bitten by a mad dog and he is dying from rabies. The doctor says that he will die tonight unless I can pay for treatment. The treatment will cost forty thousand rupees.'

'I'm sorry,' I said. 'This money is for the treatment of someone that I love. I cannot help you.'

Then I ran on into the Emergency Ward. Nita was asleep, but her father was sitting by her bed.

'Why have you come?' he asked.

'I have got the money,' I told him.

He looked at the money and said, 'Where did you steal it from?'

A Love Story

'That does not matter,' I said. 'I have come to take Nita away with me.'

'Nita is staying here,' he said. 'She is hurt badly inside her body and the doctors say it will take her four months to get well again. Her treatment will be very expensive. Sixty thousand rupees. If you really want Nita, come back with sixty thousand rupees.'

I knew then that Nita would never be mine. Her father would want more money than I could ever afford. I felt sick. I saw blackness all around me and I closed my eyes.

When I opened them again, I saw a newspaper on the floor. It had an advertisement with a picture of a man on it. The man was smiling and holding several thousand-rupee notes in his hand. The words under the picture read: *Welcome to the greatest show on television* – Who Will Win A Billion? *Call or write to us. Perhaps you will be a lucky winner!*

I looked at the address. It said: *Prem Studios, Khar, Mumbai*. I knew in that moment that I was going to Mumbai.

The man with glasses and thick black hair was waiting outside the ward. He looked at me with hopeful eyes, but he did not try to speak to me. I still had the paper bag in my hand.

'Take this,' I said, and I gave him the bag. 'There are forty thousand rupees inside. Go and save your son's life.'

The man took the bag and began crying. 'Thank you,' he said. He took a business card from his pocket. 'This is my name and address. I will pay you the money back as soon as I can. I am a teacher, but from this moment I am your servant.'

'Thank you. But I don't think I will need you,' I said. 'I'm going to Mumbai.'

―――

I am sitting on Smita's sofa with tears falling from my eyes.

'I am sorry, Ram,' she says. 'Is Nita still in Agra?'

A Love Story

'I don't know where she is,' I say. 'Will I ever see her again? I don't know.'

'Let's see the next question,' says Smita.

———

'In which Shakespeare play do we find the character Costard?' Prem Kumar asked. 'Is it a) *King Lear*, b) *The Merchant of Venice*, c) *Love's Labour's Lost* or d) *Othello*?'

I stared at him.

'Do you have an answer?' he asked.

'Not at the moment,' I replied.

'No?' he said. 'What are you going to do? You can ask me for Half and Half, or go for a Friendly Tip.'

What could I do? Who could I ask for the answer to this question? I put my hand into my shirt pocket to look for my lucky coin. Instead, I pulled out a business card. Suddenly, I remembered that it belonged to the man I had met in the hospital, the one whose son had rabies. It read: *Utpal Chatterjee, English Teacher, St John's School, Agra*. Then it gave a phone number.

I gave the card to Prem Kumar. 'Please call this man,' I said. 'I am using my Friendly Tip.'

Prem Kumar stared at the card. He had a worried look on his face, but he picked up a phone and gave it to me. 'You have two minutes,' he said. 'And your two minutes start … now.'

I phoned the number on the card and half a minute passed. The audience was watching me worriedly. Suddenly, someone said, 'Hello?'

'Hello,' I said. 'Can I speak to Mr Uptal Chatterjee?'

'This is me,' he said.

'Mr Chatterjee,' I said. 'I am Ram Mohammad Thomas. You do not know my name, but we met in Singhania Hospital. Do you remember?'

A Love Story

'Oh, my God!' he said. 'I've been searching for you. You saved my son's life. I...'

'Mr Chatterjee, I do not have much time,' I said. 'I am on a television quiz show and I need you to answer a question for me.'

'A question? Yes, of course,' he said.

Less than thirty seconds were left. Everyone was watching the clock on the wall.

'Tell me quickly, in which Shakespeare play do we find the character Costard?' I asked. 'Is it a) *King Lear*, b) *The Merchant of Venice*, c) *Love's Labour's Lost* or d) *Othello*?'

Mr Chatterjee was silent. There were only fifteen seconds left. 'I don't know,' he said. 'It is either *King Lear* or *Love's Labour's Lost*.'

'I can only give one answer,' I said.

'Then try *Love's Labour's Lost*,' he said.

'Mr Thomas, I need your answer,' said Prem Kumar. 'Your two minutes have finished.'

'It is C. *Love's Labour's Lost*,' I said.

'Are you absolutely sure of your answer?'

'Yes,' I said.

There was the sound of drums. The correct answer lit up on the screen.

'Absolutely correct!' said Prem Kumar, and he stood up. His face was red and covered in sweat. 'You have won one million rupees. How do you feel?'

'Q Bzzg Cnzxp!' I said.

'What did you say?' asked Prem Kumar.

'I said that I feel great,' I replied.

10
At Home with a Killer

I decided not to meet with Salim when I was back in Mumbai because I did not want him to know about my plan to get on to the quiz show. But one day I was walking along the street when he almost knocked me down.

'Excuse me,' he apologized, and then he recognized me.

'Mohammad!' he cried. 'What are you doing in Mumbai?'

Salim was taller and more handsome. At sixteen, he looked as good as any film star.

'I am taking acting lessons,' he told me. 'Abbas Rizvi, the famous film producer, is paying for them. He has offered me the role of the hero in his next film.'

'That's wonderful, Salim,' I said. 'How did all this happen?'

'After you went away, I continued my work delivering tiffin,' Salim said. 'One day I was collecting a tiffin from the wife of a customer called Mukesh Rawal. Mrs Rawal told me that her husband had an office job, but that sometimes he worked as a junior actor in films.

'I went to Mukesh Rawal's office and asked him about being a junior actor,' Salim went on. 'He said that I was too young. "But sometimes they have roles for street children," Rawal said. "Give me some photographs of yourself, and I'll show them to Pappu Master. He finds work for junior actors."

'I went to the photographer's shop, but his prices were too expensive. He told me to buy a cheap camera and take my own pictures. So I did. I went to different places in the city and asked people to take my picture. I got almost twenty pictures of myself. I also took some pictures of places and people. One of these was of a large, middle-aged man. I had just pushed the button when I recognized him. He also recognized me because

At Home with a Killer

the man said, "You are Salim, aren't you? You ran away from me. But you won't get away from me now!" It was Mr Babu Pillai, or Maman!'

'Oh, my God!' I cried. 'What did you do?'

'I ran away from him and jumped on a bus. Maman was just behind me. He tried to get on the bus, but a man suddenly came between us and pushed Maman off! The man's name was Ahmed Khan. I sat next to him on the bus and thanked him. He told me that he had a big house and needed someone to do the cooking and cleaning, so I became his servant.

'That week I gave my photographs to Mukesh Rawal,' Salim went on, 'and he showed them to Pappu Master. After three months, I got my first film role. I was a college student in the Abbas Rizvi film *Bad Boys*.'

'Let's go and see it now,' I said excitedly.

Salim looked down at his shoes. 'I am on screen for just three seconds and I don't speak. But I met Abbas Rizvi, and he promised to give me a bigger role in his next film.

'Ahmed Khan was crazy about cricket. He also liked to watch *Mumbai Crime Watch* on TV. Have you ever seen it?'

'No, *Mumbai Crime Watch* wasn't on the TV in Delhi or in Agra,' I said.

'It's like a news programme, but they only tell you about violent crime,' said Salim. 'It was very strange. Sometimes large yellow envelopes were delivered to Ahmed's house. One afternoon, I spilt tea on one of the envelopes. I was afraid that I had spoilt the papers inside, so I opened it.'

'What was in the envelope?' I asked.

'A photograph of a man's face and a piece of paper. The words on the paper said:

Name: Vithalbhai Ghorpade
Age: 56
Address: 73/4 Marve Road, Malad

'I guessed that he was a business friend of Ahmed's. I closed it up again quickly. That evening, Ahmed opened the envelope. Soon after, he received a phone call. "Yes, I have received it," is all that he said. Two weeks later, Ahmed was watching *Mumbai Crime Watch*. I was in the kitchen, but I could hear the man speaking on the TV. "... businessman Vithalbhai Ghorpade was shot dead in his house on Marve Road. Mr Ghorpade was fifty-six." I heard Ahmed laughing and was surprised. Why would he laugh about the murder of a business friend?

'A month later, there was another yellow envelope,' Salim went on. 'Ahmed was out, so I opened it carefully. This time, the photograph was of a young man. The words on the paper said:

Name: Jameel Kidwai
Age: 28
Address: 35 Shilajit Apartments, Colaba

Ahmed came home that evening and looked at the yellow envelope. Soon after, there was a phone call. "Yes, I have received it," he said again. A week later, I heard the news on *Mumbai Crime Watch*. A young lawyer named Jameel Kidwai had been shot dead getting out of his car near his home in Shilajit Apartments.

'I was now very worried. When the next yellow envelope arrived, I looked at the photograph and wrote down the man's address in Premier Road, in Kurla. The next day, I followed Ahmed. He went to Premier Road, but he did not enter the house. He passed it three or four times, as if he was checking it, then he went home. Two weeks later, *Mumbai Crime Watch* reported that the man had been found murdered in his home on Premier Road.

'I knew then that Ahmed was paid to kill people. What was I to do?' Salim asked. 'Ahmed had saved me from Maman, so I could not betray[72] him to the police. Then Abbas Rizvi offered me a role in his next film. But something terrible happened.'

'What?' I said.

'It was four months ago,' said Salim. 'The twentieth of February. I remember the day because of the cricket match. India was playing against Australia, and India's greatest batsman, Sachin Malvankar, was in the team. Ahmed had bet[73] ten thousand rupees that Malvankar would make his thirty-seventh test century[74] that day. I heard him on the telephone, placing the bet.'

'Did Malvankar make his thirty-seventh century?' I asked.

'No,' said Salim. 'And Ahmed lost his ten thousand rupees. He was very angry and left the house. But that same afternoon, another yellow envelope arrived. I saw the photograph inside and almost died.'

'Why?' I asked.

'It was a photograph of Abbas Rizvi,' said Salim.

'No!' I said. 'What did you do?'

'I immediately went to Rizvi and warned him,' said Salim. 'At first, he didn't believe me, but then I showed him the photograph and his address. He told me that he would run away to Dubai for a year or two. But he was very grateful to me and promised to make me a hero in his next film, and to pay for my acting lessons.

'So when I got back to the house, I put a new picture and a new address in the yellow envelope. Ahmed murdered the wrong man. But before he could discover this, I told him that I had to go to Bihar and I left his employment.

'Then last week, on *Mumbai Crime Watch*, I saw that the police had shot and killed a killer by the name of Ahmed Khan near Churchgate Station.'

'My God!' I cried. 'But what photograph and address did you put in the yellow envelope?'

'My photograph of Maman and his address,' he said.

'Very clever!' says Smita. 'But did you tell Salim about the quiz show?'

'No,' I say.

'So Salim doesn't know that you were on *Who Will Win a Billion?*' says Smita. 'Well, let's see how meeting Salim helped you with the next question.'

'This question for ten million rupees is from the world of sport,' said Prem Kumar. 'How many test centuries has India's greatest batsman Sachin Malvankar scored? Is it a) 34, b) 35, c) 36 or d) 37?'

'Can I ask a question?' I said.

'Yes,' said Prem Kumar.

'Has India played another country since they played Australia?'

'No,' said Prem Kumar. He was getting more and more nervous and kept looking at the producer.

'Then the answer is C, 36.'

'Are you absolutely sure of your answer?'

'Yes,' I said.

There was the sound of drums. The correct answer lit up on the screen.

'Absolutely correct!' said Prem Kumar. 'You have won ten million rupees.'

11
Look after your Buttons

I had been working at Jimmy's Bar and Restaurant in Mumbai for two months. It was past midnight, but the one customer at the bar didn't want to go home. The man was in his early thirties and was wearing an expensive dark suit.

'Oh, my dear brother!' he was saying. 'I am so sorry!'

The management had told us to talk with the customers, so I asked, 'What happened to your brother, Sir?'

He looked at me. 'I am Prakash Rao. Managing Director of Surya Industries,' he said. 'We make buttons for shirts, trousers, coats, skirts.'

'And your brother?' I asked. 'What is his name?'

'Arvind Rao,' he replied. 'He was the owner of Surya Industries and a great businessman. He gave me a job in his office in New York.'

'New York!' I said. 'That must have been exciting.'

'Yes,' he said. 'But I met Julie in New York.' He was silent for a moment, then he went on. 'Her real name was Erzulie De Ronceray, but everyone called her Julie. She was a cleaner in the office building. She was also an illegal immigrant[75] from Haiti.'

'Where is Haiti?' I asked.

'It's a tiny country near Mexico,' he said.

'Let me guess,' I said. 'You fell in love with Julie and married her.'

'Right!' he said. 'We went to Port Louis for our honeymoon[76]. And there I discovered that Julie practised voodoo.'

'Voodoo?' I asked 'What's that?'

'It's a religion in Haiti,' he told me. 'People who practise voodoo can do all kinds of strange things. It's a kind of magic.'

'So what happened?' I said.

'Julie was just a cleaner, but she wanted to live like a rich lady,' he said. 'She wanted money all the time. She seemed to forget she was married to the brother of the owner of a large company, not the owner himself.

'So I started stealing money from my brother's company,' he went on. 'Just a few dollars at first, but then more and more. Soon my brother noticed it. He was very angry, but he did not go to the police. Instead, he brought me back from America to a small office in Hyderabad. He ordered me to pay back half of the stolen money out of my salary.

'I was happy to do this because I didn't want to go to prison. But Julie was angry. "How can your brother do this to you?" she said. "It's cruel." And over time I started to agree with her. Arvind *had* been cruel, I told myself. He had to be punished. "Get me a button from one of your brother's unwashed shirts," Julie said. "And some of his hair." So I visited his house in Mumbai. I pulled a button from a shirt that he had taken off. Then I took some of his hair from a hairbrush in his bedroom. Back at home, Julie stuck them on to a doll. Next she killed a chicken and put the head of the doll into the chicken's blood. "Now the voodoo doll is ready," Julie said. She got a black pin and said, "Push this pin into the doll's head, and your brother will have a very bad headache. Push it into the button and he will have bad chest pains. Here, try it."

'She gave me the pin. I thought that she was playing a game, so I laughed and pushed the pin into the white button on the doll's chest. Two hours later, I received a phone call. Arvind was in hospital. He was having a heart attack.'

'That's amazing,' I cried.

'Over the next two months, I began to enjoy causing my brother pain,' Prakash Rao went on. 'I went to Mumbai and took the doll to a dinner where my brother was receiving a business award. Arvind was giving his thank-you speech with the glass award in his hands. I secretly pushed the black pin into the doll's head, soon after he started talking. "My friends, thank you for owwwwwwwwww!" He screamed and dropped the glass award. It broke into a million pieces.

'After that, my brother was locked up in a hospital for people who are mentally ill. While he was there, I became Managing Director of the company and I was soon very rich. But I also started to think about my life.'

There was a silence, then Prakash Rao went on. 'My brother died two weeks ago.' He held his head in his hands. 'Oh, my poor brother! He's dead, and I killed him.'

'I'm sorry,' I said.

Then he looked up, angrily. 'I'll send Julie back to Haiti,' he said. 'Or …' Then he smiled and took a small gun from his pocket. It was no bigger than a child's hand. 'I'll use this to kill her and … owwwwwwwwwwwwwwww!!!'

Suddenly, he screamed and put his hands on his chest. Then he fell face-down on the bar.

I did not think that he would be paying for his drink.

The police arrived after half an hour. An ambulance came with a doctor, and he told us that Prakash Rao had died from a heart attack. The police discovered a lot of money in Prakash Rao's pockets.

They did not find his gun.

Dead men don't need guns.

Smita is smiling. 'I cannot believe that Rao was killed by someone pushing a pin into a voodoo doll,' she says.

'Listen to my answer to the next question,' I say.

Smita presses 'Play'.

Look after your Buttons

'What is the capital city of Papua New Guinea?' asked Prem Kumar. 'Is it a) Port Louis, b) Port-au-Prince, c) Port Moresby or d) Port Adelaide?'

'I know that it is not Port-au-Prince, which is the capital of Haiti, or Port Louis, which is in Mauritius,' I said. 'It is also not Port Adelaide because Adelaide is in Australia. So the answer is C. Port Moresby.'

'Are you absolutely sure of your answer?' said Prem Kumar. He wiped more sweat from his forehead and looked amazed.

'Yes,' I said.

There was the sound of drums. The correct answer lit up on the screen.

'Absolutely correct!' said Prem Kumar. 'You have won one hundred million rupees. This is amazing! It's almost like magic.'

12
The Last Question

Prem Kumar looked at the camera.

'The last question,' he said. 'This is the billion-rupee question. Mumtaz Mahal was the wife of Emperor Shahjahan. He built the world-famous Taj Mahal, but what was the name of Mumtaz Mahal's father? Was it a) Mirza Ali Kuli Beg, b) Sirajuddaulah, c) Asaf Jah or d) Abdur Rahim Khan Khanan?

'Think about the answer carefully, Mr Thomas. Ladies and gentlemen, we are going to take a commercial break[77]. Please don't go away!'

The studio sign changed to 'Applause[78]' and the programme stopped recording.

Prem Kumar laughed. 'Have you studied Indian history, Mr Thomas?' he said. 'No? Then you cannot know the answer. Say goodbye to the one hundred million rupees that you have won.'

I also laughed. 'The answer is Asaf Jah,' I said.

Prem Kumar stopped laughing and his mouth fell open. 'How ... how do you know this?' he asked.

'I was a Taj Mahal guide for two years,' I told him.

His face turned pale. Then he turned and ran to the producer. They talked for some time. Ten minutes passed. The audience waited impatiently. At last Prem Kumar came back to his seat. The studio sign changed to 'Applause' and the programme began recording again.

'Ladies and gentlemen,' said Prem Kumar. 'Before the commercial break, I asked for the name of Mumtaz Mahal's father. But it was not a question at all. We were recording a commercial for Mumtaz Tea!'

The audience started to whisper to each other. Someone laughed. The studio sign changed to 'Applause' again.

I was not laughing. I knew then that this show was really produced by cheats.

The studio sign changed to 'Silence' and Prem Kumar spoke into the camera.

'Ladies and gentlemen,' said Prem Kumar. 'I am going to ask the billion-rupee question. Mr Thomas, Beethoven's Piano Sonata Number 29 is also called Hammerklavier Sonata. What key is it in? Is it a) B flat major, b) G minor, c) E flat major or d) C minor? Think about the answer carefully, Mr Thomas. We will now take another commercial break. Ladies and gentlemen, this really is very exciting. Please don't go away.'

The studio sign changed to 'Applause'. The programme stopped recording.

'I need to go to the toilet,' I said.

'Come with me,' said Prem Kumar.

———

I was in the men's toilets at the studio. Prem Kumar and I had just washed our hands. He was smiling at me. 'I'm sorry it had to end like this,' he said. 'With no money for you to take away.'

'I did not come on your show to win money.' I said. 'I came to take revenge[79].'

'Take revenge?' said Prem Kumar, looking at me in a strange way. 'Revenge on whom?'

I took a gun from my trouser pocket. It was a small gun. No bigger than a child's hand.

His eyes opened wide with shock. 'But ... but why?' he said. 'We have never met before this show.'

'You are wrong,' I said. 'We met outside Neelima Kumari's flat. It was early in the morning. You were wearing a white shirt and blue jeans and had Neelima's money in your hand. And then there is Nita.'

'Nita?' he said. 'You ... you know Nita?'

'I asked her to marry me,' I said. 'But she *has to marry you!*

His eyes opened wide with shock. 'But ... but why?' he said. 'We have never met before this show.'

Yes, you! You cut her face and hurt her so badly that she had to stay in hospital for four months.'

'How ... how did you find me?' he asked.

'I saw an advertisement for *Who Will Win a Billion?* in a newspaper in Agra,' I said. 'Your face was on the advertisement.'

'Listen, please don't shoot me!' he cried. 'I will let you win the billion rupees.'

'I am not returning to the quiz show,' I said. 'And neither are you.'

I pointed the gun at him.

In the films it looks like it is easy to kill a man. But it is not. You know that when you fire the bullet, it will go into someone's heart. Red blood will begin to pour onto the floor.

So I tried to feel angry. I tried to remember the bruises on Neelima's face and Nita's body. But instead of anger, I felt sadness. Suddenly, there were tears in my eyes, and I realized that I could not simply kill another man in cold blood[80]. Not even a rat[81] like Prem Kumar.

I put the gun back in my pocket.

'Thank you for sparing my life, Mr Thomas,' he said, wiping sweat from his forehead. 'I will tell you the answer to the last question and you will get a billion rupees!'

I did not come on to the show to win, but a billion rupees was a lot of money. With a billion rupees I could buy Nita's freedom. She would not have to marry Prem Kumar. I could make Salim a film star. I could help thousands of orphans and street children. And I could buy a big car.

Prem Kumar smiled. 'Listen carefully. The correct answer is C. Just say "C" and a billion rupees will be yours. OK?'

'OK,' I said, nodding.

We returned to the studio, and the studio sign changed to 'Silence'. The programme began again.

The Last Question

Prem Kumar turned to me. 'Mr Ram Mohammad Thomas, before the commercial break I asked you the last question. Are you ready to answer?'

'In a moment,' I said. 'I would like to use Half and Half.'

Prem Kumar looked at me worriedly and pressed a button. The screen changed and showed answers A and C.

'There you have it,' Prem Kumar said. 'It is either A or C. Give me the right answer and you will become the first man in history to win a billion rupees. Give me the wrong answer and you will become the first man in history to lose one hundred million rupees in less than a minute. What is your decision?'

I took out my lucky one-rupee coin. 'Heads my answer will be A, tails it will be C,' I said.

Prem Kumar nodded his head. There was an evil look in his eyes. I threw the coin into the air and it came down on my hand. There were gasps from the audience. They could not believe that I would gamble so much money. I looked at the coin, and it was heads.

'The answer is A,' I said.

Prem Kumar glared at me. 'Are you absolutely sure, Mr Thomas? You can still choose C if you want.'

'Yes,' I said. 'I am absolutely sure.'

'Correct!' he said, in a shaky voice. 'Mr Ram Mohammad Thomas, you have won one billion rupees!'

For almost two minutes, everyone stood and clapped. The stage was lit with many colours. I smiled at Prem Kumar. He did not smile at me. Suddenly, the producer came and took Prem Kumar outside the studio. They started shouting at each other.

Smita looks at her watch and gets up from the sofa.

'What a story!' she says. 'What a show! So Prem Kumar tried to give you the wrong answer even after you spared his life.'

The Last Question

'Now you must decide,' I tell her. 'Do I deserve the top prize? I have told you all my secrets.'

'And now I will tell you *my* secret,' she says. She looks straight into my eyes. 'I am Gudiya, the girl that you helped in the chawl. You did not kill my father. He only broke a leg. But thanks to you, he never hurt me again. I have been trying to find you for years, Ram. Then yesterday I saw your name in the newspaper. It said that you had been arrested, so I hurried to the police station.'

Tears of happiness start to fall from my eyes, and I put my arms around her.

'Gudiya,' I say. 'Now I have a lawyer, a friend and a sister.'

'You fought for me,' she says. 'Now I will fight for you.'

13
A Sister's Promise

Six months have passed, and the police have not arrested me. That was because Smita fought for me like a mother fights for her children.

She found out that the police were not looking for the person who killed a robber on the train. Nobody had even heard of the robber.

The quiz company tried to say that I was cheating, but Smita proved them wrong with the DVD. After four months, I got the prize money. Not quite a billion. The government took some. They called it a 'quiz show tax'.

The company producing *Who Will Win a Billion?* did not make any more television programmes because they had no money left. So I was the first and the last winner on the show.

Prem Kumar died two months ago. The police say that he killed himself. Perhaps he did, or perhaps the people who ran the quiz show killed him. I do not know.

Salim has got the role of a seventeen-year-old college hero in a film. He thinks that the producer is a man called Mohammad Bhatt, but it is really me.

My dearest love is with me in Mumbai. Mrs Nita Mohammad Thomas is now my wife.

Smita and I are walking along Marine Drive, by the sea. My car and its driver are following us slowly.

'I want to ask you something,' I say. 'Why didn't you tell me immediately that you were Gudiya?'

'Because I wanted to hear your stories and find out the truth,' she says. 'And I soon knew that your stories were true.'

'When?' I ask.

'When you told me *my* story, and you didn't realize that it was me listening to you,' she says. 'Now, can I ask you a question?'

'Of course,' I say.

'Why did you throw up a coin the evening that I first brought you home?' Smita asks.

'I was asking myself, "Can I trust her?"' I explain. 'So I let my lucky coin decide. Heads I was going to tell you everything, tails I was going to say goodbye.'

'So you believe in luck,' she says.

I smile. 'No. Look at the coin.' I take it from my pocket and give it to her.

She looks at it and turns it over. 'It ... it's got heads on both sides!'

'Yes,' I say. 'It's my lucky coin – but I don't believe in luck.'

I take the coin from her and throw it into the air. It goes up, up and up, then drops down into the sea.

'Why did you throw it away?' she asks.

'I don't need it any more,' I say. 'Because luck comes from inside a person.'

'I don't need it any more,' I say.
'Because luck comes from inside a person.'

Points for Understanding

1

1. Where was Ram at the start of this chapter?
2. Why was Inspector Godbole beating Ram?
3. Why was Ram surprised to see Smita Shah?
4. Later, Smita and Ram watched the DVD of the quiz show. Why did Ram agree to do this and what did Smita want to find out?

2

1. Father Timothy gave the orphan boy three names. What were they and how would these names help the boy?
2. What did Ram learn when he was living with Father Timothy?
3. Father Timothy told Ram something that made him very sad. What was it?
4. Who was Prem Kumar and why did he change the first question in *Who Will Win a Billion*?
5. How did Ram know the answer to the first question?

3

1. Ram did not like the Delhi Children's Home for Boys, but some other boys did. Why was that?
2. How were Ram and his new friend, Salim, like each other?
3. What did the boys find out from the fortune-teller? What did he give Ram?
4. Who was Sethji and why did he visit the Children's Home?
5. What did the boys learn about Sethji on the train to Mumbai?
6. 'I was sure that this was the best thing that had ever happened to me.' What was Ram talking about?
7. Why were Ram and Salim really having singing lessons?
8. What did Ram and Salim do when they learnt the truth?

4

1. Neelima Kumari had been a very famous film actress. What did she have in her flat to remind her of that?
2. What changed after Neelima's mother died?
3. How did Ram find out that Neelima had a lover?
4. What did Neelima's lover look like and what kind of man was he?
5. What was Neelima's 'greatest role'?

5

1. Who was Balwant Singh and what did he look like?
2. He talks about a war. When was it and which countries were fighting each other?
3. Balwant Singh told some heroic stories, but they were not true. How did everyone find this out?
4. What was the truth about Balwant Singh?
5. How did the old soldier's stories help Ram with the answer to the next quiz question?

6

1. What was Mr Ramakrishna's job? Did he do it well? Explain your answer.
2. Describe the boys' new neighbours.
3. Mr Shantaram's daughter, Gudiya, had a cat. Why did she call it Pluto?
4. Why did Gudiya have to go to hospital?
5. Ram made Gudiya a promise after she left hospital. What was it and how did he keep it?
6. Ram left _____ and went to _____ . Why?

7

1. The Taylors were Australian. What were they doing in Delhi?
2. Why was Colonel Taylor called 'The Man Who Knows'?
3. What was the secret of the Colonel's Den and how did Ram discover it?
4. Why did Colonel Taylor have to leave Delhi?
5. Who do you think phoned the inspector about Colonel Taylor and Jeevan Kumar?

8

1. What did Ram take with him when he left Delhi?
2. Where was his salary from the Taylors and why?
3. Who was the young man with the beard and what did he want?
4. 'Fifty thousand dreams had suddenly been taken from me.' What did Ram mean?
5. What happened to the robber and his gun?
6. Which of these sentences is true: (a) Ram wanted to go to Mumbai, but he got on the wrong train. (b) Ram was afraid to go to Mumbai. (c) Ram had planned to go to Agra?

9

1. Where did Ram live in Agra and who helped him find the place?
2. Ram's new friend had a problem, but he was not mentally disabled. Explain your answer.
3. Ram soon had a job. What did he do and how did he learn the things he needed to know for the job?
4. Ram and Nita fell in love. But why could they not get married?
5. Why did Ram ask Swapna Devi for forty thousand rupees?
6. What happened to Shankar and what did Ram do as a result?
7. Why was Nita in hospital?
8. Why did Ram need forty thousand rupees for the second time?
9. How did he get the money?
10. Why did Ram decide to go to Mumbai?
11. Why did Ram give money to the man in the hospital and what was he given in return?

10

1. Where did Ram meet his friend Salim?
2. Explain how Salim had become a junior actor.
3. How did Salim meet Maman?
4. How did Ahmed Khan help Salim?
5. What did Salim find out about Ahmed Khan?
6. How did Salim and Abbas Rizvi help each other?
7. What happened to Maman in the end?
8. What happened to Ahmed Khan and how did Salim find out about it?
9. How did Salim's story help Ram with the next question?

11

1. Who told Ram about some different countries around the world?
2. Where did Prakash Rao meet his wife and where was she from?
3. What is voodoo and in which country do people usually practise it?
4. Who taught Prakash Rao how to practise voodoo?
5. What happened to Prakash Rao's brother?
6. What was Prakash Rao planning to do?
7. What happened to him?
8. Why did the police not find his gun?

12

1. Why did Prem Kumar say that they were recording a commercial for tea?
2. Ram told Prem Kumar that he wanted revenge, not money. Explain what he meant.
3. Why did Ram put the gun back in his pocket and go back to finish the quiz?
4. Why did Ram choose the answer A?
5. What was Smita's secret?

13

1. How did Smita help Ram?
2. Ram did not get exactly one billion rupees. Why not?
3. How did Prem Kumar die?
4. How did Ram help his friend Salim?
5. Where was Ram living at the end of the story and who was he living with?
6. What was unusual about Ram's lucky coin?
7. Ram said that luck came from inside a person. Explain what he meant.

Glossary

1 **psychology** (page 4)
   the study of the mind and how it affects behaviour
2 **philosophy** (page 4)
   the study of theories about the meaning of things such as life, knowledge and beliefs
3 **diplomat** (page 4)
   an official whose job is to represent their government in a foreign country
4 **accused** – *to accuse someone* (page 5)
   to say that someone has done something wrong or committed a crime
5 **hosted** – *to host something* (page 5)
   to introduce and talk to the people taking part in a television or radio programme
6 **charity** (page 5)
   an organization to which you give money so that it can give money and help to people who are poor or ill, or who need advice and support
7 **priest** (page 5)
   someone whose job is to perform ceremonies and other duties in some Christian churches
8 **slum** (page 5)
   a poor area of a town where the houses are in very bad condition
9 **monsoon** (page 6)
   a period of heavy rain in India and South-East Asia
10 **nominated** – *to nominate someone or something* (page 6)
   to officially suggest that someone should be given a job, or that someone or something should receive a prize
11 **beam** (page 10)
   a long thick piece of wood, metal or concrete that supports a roof
12 **arrest** (page 12)
   if the police *arrest* someone, they take that person to a police station because they believe he or she has committed a crime. This situation is called *arrest*.
13 **fainted** – *to faint* (page 12)
   to suddenly be in a condition similar to sleep in which you do not see, feel or think, and fall to the ground

14 **heads** (page 12)
the side of a coin that has a picture of a head on it. The other side is *tails*.
15 **orphanage** (page 13)
a building where *orphans* – children whose parents have died – live and are looked after. A place where children can be sent to live if they cannot live with their family is called a *children's home*.
16 **Jesus** (page 13)
the man on whose ideas Christianity is based. Christians believe he was the son of God.
17 **altar** (page 13)
a special table where religious ceremonies are performed, especially in a Christian church. In many churches there is a *crucifix* above the *altar*, which is a model of Jesus.
18 **presenter** (page 14)
the person who introduces a television or radio programme
19 **disabled** (page 16)
someone who is *disabled* is unable to use part of their body or brain properly because of injury or disease
20 **warden** (page 16)
someone whose job is to be responsible for a particular place or thing, and who checks that rules are obeyed
21 **deputy** (page 16)
someone whose job is the second most important in a department or organization, and who takes the responsibilities of the most important person in some situations
22 **big wheel** (page 17)
a machine at a fair or park in the shape of a large *wheel* with seats on the edge, that takes people round and round in the air
23 **booth** (page 17)
a small enclosed space where you can buy things, look at things or use a service
24 **fortune-teller** (page 17)
someone who looks at your hand, a special set of cards etc in order to tell you what is going to happen to you in the future
25 **gangster** (page 18)
a member of an organized group of criminals called a *gang*
26 **basement** (page 21)
the part of a building that is partly or completely below the level of the ground

27 *punished* – *to punish someone* (page 21)
   to make someone suffer because they have done something against the law or against the rules
28 *beggar* (page 22)
   someone who is very poor and lives by asking people for money or food. To ask people for money or food is to *beg*.
29 *blind* (page 22)
   unable to see
30 *praising* – *to praise someone* (page 23)
   to show your love of a God with words or music
31 *queen* (page 26)
   a woman who does something very well. Neelima was very good at acting in *tragedies* – plays or films in which people suffer or die, especially one in which the main character dies at the end. That is why she was called the *Tragedy Queen*.
32 *comedy* (page 27)
   a funny film, play or television programme
33 *role* (page 27)
   the character played by a particular actor in a film, play etc
34 *bruise* (page 29)
   a mark that you get on your body if you are hit or if you knock against something
35 *foundry* (page 30)
   a factory where metal or glass is heated and made into different objects
36 *air raid* (page 32)
   an *attack* – a violent attempt to harm a person, animal or place – in which one or more planes drop bombs
37 *siren* (page 32)
   a piece of equipment that makes a loud sound, used for warning people
38 *airfield* (page 33)
   a place where aircraft arrive and leave, especially military or private aircraft
39 *regiment* (page 33)
   a group of soldiers that can be divided into smaller groups called *battalions* and whose leader is called a *colonel*
40 *bunker* (page 33)
   a room or set of rooms with very strong walls, built underground as a shelter against bombs or enemy soldiers

41 **cremate** – *to cremate someone* (page 33)
   to burn the body of a dead person
42 **rocket** (page 33)
   a weapon shaped like a tube that flies through the air and explodes when it hits something. These weapons are fired from a *rocket launcher*.
43 **exploded** – *to explode* (page 33)
   to burst with a lot of force and a loud noise. When something *explodes*, there is an *explosion*.
44 **wound** (page 33)
   an injury in which your skin is damaged, usually seriously
45 **launching** – *to launch something* (page 33)
   to send a rocket, satellite or other object into the air or into space
46 **bayonet** (page 34)
   a long sharp blade that is fixed onto the end of a long gun
47 **the armed forces** (page 34)
   a country's army, navy and air force
48 **tank** (page 35)
   a very strong military vehicle with a large gun on the top and wheels that have metal bands around them
49 **bomb** (page 35)
   a weapon made to explode at a particular time or when it hits something
50 **bullet** (page 35)
   a small piece of metal that is shot from a gun and causes serious damage to the person or thing it hits
51 **sympathy** (page 39)
   a natural feeling of kindness and understanding that you have for someone who is experiencing something very difficult
52 **railing** (page 40)
   a fence made of narrow posts supporting an upper bar
53 **astronomer** (page 40)
   someone who studies the stars and planets using scientific equipment including a *telescope* – a piece of equipment shaped like a tube that you look through to make distant objects look closer and larger
54 **bandage** (page 42)
   a long, thin piece of cloth that you wrap around an injured part of your body

55 *interfere* – *to interfere in something* (page 43)
   to become involved in a situation and try to influence the way that it develops, although you have no right to do this
56 *hang* – *to hang someone* (page 45)
   to kill someone by putting a rope around their neck and making them fall
57 *sacked* – *to sack someone* (page 46)
   to tell someone that they can no longer work at their job
58 *den* (page 46)
   a room in a house where someone goes to be alone
59 **Ministry of Defence** (page 49)
   a government department that is responsible for protecting their country
60 *broke into* – *to break into something* (page 50)
   to enter a building by force, especially in order to steal things
61 *spying* – *to spy* (page 50)
   to find out secret information about what a country or an organization is doing
62 *acceptable* (page 53)
   good enough for a particular purpose or situation
63 *berth* (page 55)
   a bed on a train or ship
64 *revolver* (page 56)
   a small gun that holds several bullets
65 *stain* (page 57)
   a mark left accidentally on clothes or surfaces
66 *outhouse* (page 62)
   a building near to a house or joined on to it, traditionally used for storing things
67 *mentally* (page 62)
   existing in the mind. Someone who is *mentally disabled* is not able to learn or develop skills at the same rate as most other people because they have a problem with their brain.
68 *engaged* (page 64)
   if two people are *engaged*, they have formally agreed to get married
69 *rabies* (page 66)
   a very serious disease that makes an animal or a human feel crazy. Humans get it only if they are bitten by an animal with *rabies*.

70 **dare** – *to dare do something* (page 68)
if you *dare* to do something, you are not afraid to do it, even though it may be dangerous or shocking or may cause trouble for you. *How dare you/he/she/they* is used for saying how shocked and angry you are about something that someone has done or said.

71 **safe** (page 68)
a strong metal box with a special lock, used for storing valuable things

72 **betray** – *to betray someone* (page 76)
if you *betray* someone, you do something to hurt them

73 **bet** – *to bet* (page 76)
to risk an amount of money by saying what you think will happen, especially in a race or game. You lose the money if you are wrong and win more if you are right. Another word with the same meaning is *gamble*.

74 **century** (page 76)
a score of one hundred points made in cricket by one player

75 **immigrant** (page 78)
someone who comes to live in a country from another country

76 **honeymoon** (page 78)
a holiday that two people take after they get married

77 **commercial break** (page 82)
a short pause in a television or radio programme when advertisements are shown

78 **applause** (page 82)
the sound made by people hitting the palms of their hands together after a performance, speech etc to show they have enjoyed it

79 **revenge** (page 83)
something that you do to hurt or punish someone because they have hurt you or someone close to you

80 **in cold blood** (page 85)
in a cruel, calm way, without showing any emotion

81 **rat** (page 85)
someone who is not honest or who tricks people

Definitions adapted from the Macmillan English Dictionary *2nd Edition © Macmillan Publishers Limited 2007*
www.macmillandictionaries.com

Exercises

Background Information

Choose the correct information to complete the sentences.

1 Vikas Swarup grew up in Mumbai / (Allahabad).
2 He has worked as a diplomat / director in many countries.
3 He spent two years / months writing the book.
4 The quiz show that the book is based on was first shown in Britain / India.
5 Mumbai has a very large number of poor / rich people.
6 Ram Mohammad Thomas is poor / educated.
7 The film of *Slumdog Millionaire* was made in 2009 / 2008.
8 The film was directed by an Indian / a British man.
9 The film won ten / eight Oscars.

People in the Story

Write a name next to the correct information below.

| Nita | Balwant Singh | Salim | ~~Smita~~ | Father Timothy | Maman |
| Neelima Kumari | Shankar | Colonel Taylor | Prem Kumar | Gudiya |

1	Smita	was Ram's lawyer.
2		took Ram to live with him when he was a young child.
3		was the TV presenter.
4		left the children's home in Delhi with Ram.

5		owned the school for disabled children.
6		was a famous actress who Ram worked for.
7		was an old soldier who told stories about a war.
8		was a young friend of Ram's. He helped her.
9		worked in India for the Australian government.
10		was the son of Swapna Devi.
11		was the girl Ram loved.

Places and Events in the Story

What happened in these places? Match the information.

1	The Church of St Mary, Delhi	Ram met Gudiya.
2	The school for disabled children, Mumbai	Ram worked for the Taylor family.
3	Juhu, Mumbai	Ram met Nita at the Taj Mahal.
4	The chawl, Mumbai	Ram and Salim had singing lessons.
5	Delhi	Ram took part in the quiz show.
6	On the train to Mumbai	Baby Ram was found on Christmas Day.
7	Agra	Ram worked for Neelima Kumari.
8	Prem Studios, Mumbai	Ram killed a robber.

Multiple Choice

Tick the best answer.

1 How did Ram know the answers to the questions on the quiz show?
   a He was lucky. ✓
   b He guessed the answers.
   c He was given the answers.
   d He cheated.

2 Where did Ram spend the first two years of his life?
   a He lived with his mother.
   b He lived with Father Timothy.
   c He lived in the Church of St Mary.
   d He lived in the St Mary's Church orphanage.

3 Why did Ram become the leader at Delhi Children's Home for Boys?
   a He was good friends with the deputy warden.
   b He spoke English.
   c He was bigger than the other boys.
   d He could sing well.

4 Why was Ram worried after Neelima Kumari's death?
   a He could not pay the rent.
   b He did not have a job.
   c He thought the police would arrest him.
   d He thought Neelima's lover would find him.

5 What did Balwant Singh lie about?
   a Receiving awards.
   b Being a soldier in the war.
   c Having a new baby son.
   d Being a war hero.

6 Why did Mr Shantaram leave his job at the Space Research Institute?
   a Because he made an important discovery.
   b Because his colleague made an important discovery.
   c Because he became very upset and angry with his colleague.
   d Because his wife told him to do another job.

7 How did Colonel Taylor know his servants were stealing from him?
   a He asked his daughter to watch them.
   b He employed people to watch them.
   c He hid cameras in their rooms.
   d He followed them.

8 Why couldn't Ram and Nita get married?
   a She was already promised to another man.
   b They were not old enough.
   c Nita wanted to wait.
   d Nita did not love Ram.

9 How did Ram discover that Swapna Devi was Shankar's mother?
   a He could understand Shankar's strange language.
   b He found pictures of Swapna Devi in Shankar's notebook.
   c Lajwanti told him all about Swapna Devi.
   d Swapna Devi told everyone at a dinner party.

10 What did Salim discover about Ahmed Khan?
   a He was a friend of Maman's.
   b He killed people for money.
   c He was a good cricket player.
   d He knew Abbas Rizvi very well.

11 Where did Ram get a gun from?
   a From a man who died in the place where he worked.
   b From the manager of Jimmy's Bar and Restaurant.
   c From the police, who left it in Jimmy's Bar and Restaurant.
   d From a woman who practised voodoo.

12 Why did Ram want to be on the quiz show?
   a He wanted to win the money.
   b Prem Kumar was his hero.
   c He wanted to punish Prem Kumar.
   d He wanted to become famous.

Vocabulary: Anagrams

Write the letters in the correct order to make words from the story.

1	EREUP	*rupee*	Indian money
2	RASI		a traditional Indian dress for women
3	STIPER		someone who works in some Christian churches
4	DONFURY		a metal or glass factory
5	DEYMOC		a funny film, play or television programme
6	GEGARB		someone who asks for money on the street to live
7	SARBIE		a disease humans can catch if they are bitten by an animal
8	DRATEGY		a film, play or television programme in which people suffer
9	PLUSAPAE		the sound made by people who have enjoyed something
10	VELERVOR		a small gun
11	CASK		to tell someone that they can no longer work at their job
12	TEEMARC		to burn the body of a dead person
13	ATSIN		a mark left accidentally on clothes or surfaces
14	NRGILIA		a fence made of narrow posts

Words from the Story

Complete the gaps. Use each word from the box once.

> immigrant   monsoon   blind   accused   slums
> diplomat   arrest   commercial   punished   ~~orphan~~
> presenter   charity   heads and tails   safe

1 Ram did not know his parents. He was an _orphan_.

2 Many people do not have good living conditions in Mumbai. They live in _____.

3 Mumbai has a big problem with water, especially in the _____ season.

4 The two sides of a coin are called _____.

5 Colonel Taylor represented the Australian government in India. He was a _____.

6 Swapna Devi put some money and a photograph in a special place called a _____.

7 Maman _____ the children who did not earn enough money.

8 Some organizations help street children. This type of organization is called a _____.

9 Surdas was a very famous singer who could not see. He was _____.

10 Prem Kumar asked the questions on the quiz show. He was the _____.

11 Before the billion-rupee question, there were two _____ breaks.

12 Julie was born in Haiti but lived in the USA. She was an _____.

13 The television company _____ Ram of cheating.

14 Ram wanted the police to _____ Neelima's boyfriend for hitting her.

Vocabulary: War

Complete each space with a letter to make a word from the story.

1 The people in the chawl knew it was dangerous to be outside because they heard the a _i_ _r_ _r_ _a_ _i_ d warning siren.
2 In the war, Balwant Singh was in a group of soldiers called a r_ _ _ _ _ t.
3 When there were explosions, the soldiers had to hide in b_ _ _ rs under the ground.
4 The b_ _ _ ts shot from guns killed many people.
5 A lot of soldiers had bad w_ _ ds and they had to be taken to hospital.
6 Balwant Singh drove a t_ _k across the bridge.

Pronunciation: Vowel sounds

Write the words in the correct columns according to the underlined vowel sounds.

~~honeymoon~~   n<u>o</u>minate   att<u>a</u>ck   g<u>a</u>mble   c<u>e</u>ntury
sl<u>u</u>m   b<u>u</u>nker   b<u>e</u>t   p<u>u</u>nish   g<u>a</u>ngster   b<u>o</u>mb
b<u>e</u>ggar   rev<u>e</u>nge   psych<u>o</u>logy   s<u>a</u>ck

b<u>a</u>d /æ/	l<u>o</u>ve /ʌ/	b<u>e</u>d /e/	h<u>o</u>t /ɒ/
	honeymoon		

Grammar: Present perfect and past simple

Choose the correct verb form, the present perfect or the past simple, to complete Ram's life story.

1. I (lived) / have lived with Father Timothy until I was eight years old.
2. I met / have met many kind people in my life, but some very bad people, too.
3. Salim was / has been my best friend since I met him at the Delhi Children's Home for Boys.
4. We stayed / have stayed together until I thought that I had killed Gudiya's father.
5. Then I ran / have run away.
6. I had / have had many different jobs.
7. I worked / have worked in a factory, as a tour guide and in a bar.
8. I was / have been a servant …
9. … and learnt / have learnt a lot from my bosses.
10. For example, Neelima, a famous actress taught / has taught me about films.
11. All my experiences helped / have helped me to be in the position I am in today.
12. Now I am very happy. I found / have found my old friend Gudiya,
13. I married / have married the girl I love …
14. … and I helped / have helped my friend Salim to become a film star.

Grammar: Prepositions

Write the correct preposition in the gap: *about*, *for* or *at*

1 A man went around town to collect money _____*for*_____ a soldiers' charity.
2 Neelima prepared _____ the greatest role of her life.
3 Prem Kumar lied _____ the answer to the final question.
4 Shantaram screamed _____ his wife and daughter.
5 At first, Ram was very excited _____ going to the new school in Mumbai.
6 Ram worked _____ Colonel Taylor.
7 Maman punished the boys _____ not making enough money.
8 Prem Kumar did not smile _____ Ram at the end of the show.
9 The fortune-teller looked _____ Ram's hand.
10 Colonel Taylor knew _____ things that happened behind closed doors.

Macmillan Readers

www.macmillanenglish.com/readers

- **Students' section** featuring *The Book Corner Club*, for those students who want to study Readers in a book club. It also features tips for creative writing and essays, a level test, webquests and URLs for further reading, articles, interviews with authors, audio, poetry and author biography worksheets
- **Teachers' section** with expanded collection of free support material including worksheets, answer keys, sample chapters, sample audio, webquests, author data sheets and the *Using Graded Readers in the Classroom* guide

MACMILLAN READERS

Macmillan Education
4 Crinan Street
London N1 9XW
A division of Springer Nature Limited
Companies and representatives throughout the world

ISBN 978-1-3800-4159-3
ISBN 978-1-3800-4109-8 (with CD edition)

Copyright © Vikas Swarup 2005. First published in the UK by Transworld Publishers, a division of The Random House Group Ltd.

This version of *Slumdog Millionaire* by Vikas Swarup was retold by John Escott for Macmillan Readers.

The authors have asserted their rights to be identified as the authors of this work in accordance with the Copyright, Design and Patents Act 1988.
Text, design and illustration © Springer Nature Limited 2019
First published 2010

This edition published 2019

All rights reserved; no part of this publication may be reproduced, stored in a retrieval system, transmitted in any form, or by any means, electronic, mechanical, photocopying, recording, or otherwise, without the prior written permission of the publishers.

Illustrated by Peter Harper and Zakir Hussein
Cover photograph by FoxSearch/Everett/Rex Features, with kind permission from Celador Films
Author photograph by Aparna Swarup

These materials may contain links for third party websites. We have no control over, and are not responsible for, the contents of such third party websites. Please use care when accessing them.
The inclusion of any specific companies, commercial products, trade names or otherwise does not constitute or imply its endorsement or recommendation by Springer Nature Limited.

Printed and bound in Great Britain by Bell and Bain Ltd, Glasgow

without CD edition

2023 2022 2021 2020 2019
10 9 8 7 6 5 4 3 2 1

with CD edition

2023 2022 2021 2020 2019
10 9 8 7 6 5 4 3 2 1